"Look at that gorgeous moon."

"I'd rather look at the gorgeous girl standing next to me," Charlie said softly.

"The…the what?" Rose tilted her head back and studied him. He didn't flinch.

"You heard me, Rose," he replied, taking her hand and leading her away from the house. "You're the prettiest girl I've ever known. You're smart and clever and wonderful. I've admired you from the first time we met."

She didn't say anything, and for a moment he wasn't sure she'd ever respond. "And you've been a wonderful friend, Charlie," she finally whispered. "Someone I can talk to about almost anything…about anyone…including Joe."

She couldn't have been clearer about her feelings. But his D-day had arrived.

"Are you going to mourn Joe for the rest of your life? I would be honored, Rose, if you'd marry me. I would be honored to be your husband. Let's you and I make a life together—and give Susan a daddy."

She stepped back, tears trickling down her face. "Marrying you is not fair. Not fair to *you*."

His heart began to sing. "I'll take that chance."

Dear Reader,

The Soldier and the Rose was born after my mother-in-law handed me a stack of wartime correspondence she had retyped from the V-mail my father-in-law had sent her. She had assigned herself this project and spent many months straining her eyes to see the small print. Her effort was truly a labor of love.

So what was in the letters between a young wife waiting at home and a husband on the front lines of Europe? As you might guess, most of the content focused on everyday life. Her letters were about their friends, neighbors and relatives. They were about the weather and stretching war coupons, sugar and meat. And, of course, she wrote about their son—my husband. The letters from the front were about mail call, the monotony of a soldier's life, mail call, the opening of the post exchange, mail call and how he missed her.

One letter stayed with me. In it, he described a rest camp located in a huge three-storied barn where he stayed for twenty-four hours and slept on a real mattress. It had soft lights, scatter rugs, easy chairs and a radio. He says, "The radio is playing 'If I Had a Talking Picture of You' and, gosh, how I wish I could have one of you."

That setting, coupled with the soldier's yearning, haunted me until it became not only my father-in-law's story but the story of *The Soldier and the Rose* in a celebration of love everlasting. Enjoy!

My best wishes,

Linda Barrett

P.S. It is such a pleasure to hear from readers. Please write to me at linda@linda-barrett.com or P.O. Box 841934, Houston, TX 77284-1934. Check out my Web site, www.linda-barrett.com, to enter contests, read excerpts and find out what's new.

The Soldier and the Rose

LINDA BARRETT

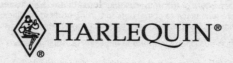

HARLEQUIN®

TORONTO • NEW YORK • LONDON
AMSTERDAM • PARIS • SYDNEY • HAMBURG
STOCKHOLM • ATHENS • TOKYO • MILAN • MADRID
PRAGUE • WARSAW • BUDAPEST • AUCKLAND

ISBN-13: 978-0-373-65421-5
ISBN-10:   0-373-65421-9

THE SOLDIER AND THE ROSE

ABOUT THE AUTHOR

Linda has been writing for pleasure all her adult life, but she targeted a professional career when she moved to Houston ten years ago. There she joined a local chapter of Romance Writers of America and attended so many workshops and seminars, "I could have had a master's degree by now," she says. Five years later, in 2001, Harlequin Superromance published her debut novel, *Love, Money and Amanda Shaw*. When not writing, the wife and mother of three grown sons (all hero material like their dad) helps develop programs for a social service agency that works with the homeless.

Books by Linda Barrett

HARLEQUIN SUPERROMANCE

★Pilgrim Cove

In memory of my father, Emanuel Cohen, and my father-in-law, John Berkowitz, who, like many others of the "greatest generation," fought in a world war so the rest of us could have a better life.

Also, in memory of my mother, Blanche, and in honor of my lively mother-in-law, Dee, who waited for their men to come home, so they could start the rest of their lives.

But mostly, this story is dedicated to those soldiers who never made it back.

And to those who mourned them.

PART ONE

Brooklyn

Chapter 1

"Love is not for cowards."

Rose Shapiro whispered the words with conviction as she sewed another row of sequins onto the new ivory silk jacket she'd wear the following evening. Ivory silk. Appropriate for celebrating a sixtieth wedding anniversary, and so different from the plain navy suit she'd worn to the wedding. She closed her eyes, shutting out that memory, shutting out the pain and confusion that accompanied her second marriage. Her marriage to Charlie.

Love is not for cowards. She understood that now, but she hadn't in the beginning when Joe had been the love of her life, and cotton-candy dreams beckoned them as they said their I do's. She'd grown up a lot since then.

She sighed and opened her eyes, once again stitching carefully. Not many couples reached sixty years of marriage. But she and Charlie had. She knotted and cut her thread, then viewed her efforts with a critical eye.

Cataract surgery last year had turned out to be a boon to her sewing skills, not that she'd thought of sewing as an art form. Using a needle had been a measure of economy during her girlhood, and she hadn't been able to break the habit later on when her pockets were fuller. Especially not with the prices of manufactured goods. In amused tones, her three children had blamed her "Depression mentality."

"The jacket is beautiful, Rosie mine," came a warm voice from the bedroom doorway. "But not as beautiful as you."

"Maybe it's your turn to have a cataract removed." She glanced playfully at Charlie's sparkling green eyes, also noting his recent haircut. Her man of sixty years was ready to party.

"There's nothing wrong with my vision," he replied, reaching for her hand. "Come on, sweetheart. It's time to practice our moves. Don't want to make fools of ourselves on the dance floor tomorrow night."

No chance of that—at least not when she was wrapped in Charlie's arms—but she didn't argue. She replaced the jacket on the padded hanger and stepped toward him.

"Ah, Rosie…" He held her close and began to hum "La Vie En Rose." *Her* song. He'd been singing it to her in two languages ever since they got married…after the war. In fact, Charlie had been romancing her since he'd met her. She hadn't always appreciated it; he wasn't Joe.

But they'd gotten past that, although not easily and not quickly. Which was why she'd planned a special surprise for Charlie tomorrow.

She kissed him on the cheek, inhaling his woodsy cologne. "Mmm…I've always loved that fragrance."

"You think I don't know?" His laughter was deep and carefree. "Life is good, Rosie, huh?"

"As good as possible for a couple of creaky octogenarians," she replied. She had no complaints, except…

Love is not for cowards.

Her heart lurched. If she was blinking rapidly now to stave off tears, they were not for herself, but for her beloved granddaughter and the young husband who adored her. Pregnant Elizabeth. Devoted Matthew. Matthew—who was about to be deployed to Iraq.

She inhaled deeply. Gathered her thoughts. The children would have to find their own way, of course, but the irony struck Rose, who'd been in the same position—pregnant with Susan, Elizabeth's mother, when Joe shipped out.

Keeping silent would kill Rose now. But she would not turn Liz's phantom worries into concrete reality. When Joe died, Rose had fallen apart; Liz didn't need to hear the details. Matthew would *not* die. At least, he probably wouldn't.

She would not have Liz thinking Charlie was second best in Rose's eyes. He didn't deserve that. War was war. Some returned and some didn't, and life had to begin again. *God help them all.*

She smiled up at Charlie and reaffirmed her original answer. "Life is good, Charlie. Very good."

Her voice quivered this time, and he squeezed her hand. "Matt's a doctor. He won't be on the front lines."

"You a mind reader?"

"Only with you." He kissed her quickly and added, "Paul drove over. He and I are going for a walk. Want to join us?"

A leisurely stroll with Charlie and their son-in-law tempted Rose, but she hesitated.

"It's a gorgeous autumn day," Charlie cajoled.

"I need to press my fancy-schmancy suit. Can't show up with more wrinkles than I have to!"

But that wasn't the real reason she stayed behind. The past had taken hold. Visual memories. Sense memories. Battles. Letters. Tears. Weddings. Children. And laughter, too. A kaleidoscope of her eighty-five years. Maybe preparations for the anniversary party had evoked them. Maybe Matthew's looming deployment… She'd certainly been maudlin since the day Liz and Matthew had announced their pregnancy last month right in the living room of Rose's Long Island home.

"We're very happy," Liz had said to the assembled family. "We both want children, and the timing's lousy, but…" She lifted her chin, her dark eyes burning.

Fear turned her granddaughter inside out. Rose saw it, heard it, and took a shaky breath. Pregnant! Rose's head pounded, and her heartbeat ricocheted. *Been there, done that, my darling girl. And survived.* But she didn't want her sweet Lizzy to suffer that same heartache.

Keep your wits about you, Rosie. The children need you. But the children had been focused only on each other at that moment, just as she and Joe had been lost in each other before he went off to war.

She'd glanced at her daughter. Pale, too pale. Susan had never met Joe, her natural father, and although she loved Charlie deeply, she'd never forgotten that fact. Her eyes had flashed with anger—her daughter pregnant and Matt deployed—but Susan had merely shifted closer to Paul and remained quiet.

"Nothing will happen to me," Matthew had declared, placing a serious kiss on his wife's mouth. "I love you, Liz, with everything I've got, but I owe Uncle Sam for my education, and after a year in the Middle East, I'll be stateside again."

"I know," Liz had whispered, snuggling closer to Matt.

"God willing," Rose had uttered at the same time. She repeated the words silently now as she smoothed her long skirt before going to her walk-in closet. She turned on the light, hung the new suit and reached overhead for a familiar, large rosewood box. Carefully wrapped in plastic, it was a six-sided piece with a silver filagree knob in the center of the cover and a garland of roses inlaid around the edge. Rose polished the wood as regularly as she did her furniture; the rich patina glowed.

The Dream Box. Originally intended as a kind of hope chest, it now held her personal history—reminders of her joy and pain. Even sixty years with a good man couldn't erase all the pain. In the end, however, it didn't matter because somehow, together, she and Charlie had become one.

She carried the Dream Box to the desk she'd brought from her parents' house, and carefully set it down. With a trembling hand, she lifted the lid and reached inside.

Chapter 2

Ani l'dodi v'dodi li—"I am my beloved's
and my beloved is mine."
—*Song of Songs*

*In the tradition of our ancestors we invite
you to join us for the wedding of our
children*

*Rose Leah
and
Joseph Abraham*

*Sunday,
December 7, 1941
12:00 p.m.*

*At the bride's home:
225 Hewes Street
Brooklyn, New York*

*Anna and Shimon Kaufman
Fanny and Mendel Rabinowitz*

Rose had written every single invitation by hand. Enough for the whole family, enough for the whole neighborhood. Her papa and mama had no money to splurge on printed invitations—no one she knew did—but Rose had the energy and desire to mark the once-in-a-lifetime occasion. So, with her fine-pointed fountain pen, a supply of India ink and plain white paper, she'd become a scribe for her own wedding. Then she'd personally delivered every one of the invitations to the aunts, uncles, cousins—the whole *mishpocha*—in Williamsburg, Brooklyn.

And now they were all here, gathering downstairs in the big living room and in the hallway—anywhere space allowed on the street-level floor of her family's brownstone.

She hadn't seen Joe yet and wouldn't before the ceremony, not that she was superstitious. Not really. But on her wedding day, she'd do nothing to invite bad luck, and remained out of sight in the upstairs bedroom she shared with her sisters.

She started to hum, then sway, then waltz around the bedroom. "'You'd...be...so easy to love...'" Not a great voice, but today she would sing.

Joe! Her heart raced as she thought about him. She loved that man, so thankful her friend Sarah had an older brother. So delighted that Joe had *finally* viewed her in that special way girls dreamed about.

Rose had noticed him years before. He was everything a girl could want—well educated, handsome, funny and respected. A professional man—

steady and reliable. Teaching high-school English meant a paycheck they could count on—and needed—because Rose, at twenty, had two more years of college ahead of her before she could contribute. Rose's family was as poor as everyone else's in the neighborhood, but all the Kaufman kids went to college. "For a good future," her papa would say, "not like now." The City University was free, a bonus for living in New York and earning good grades in high school.

"Dum…dee…dum…dum…all others above…" She grasped the bedpost and continued to sway and hum "So Easy to Love." So right! Joe and Rose. Rose and Joe. *Mrs.* Joseph Abraham Rabinowitz. Lucky, lucky… A lifetime together wouldn't be enough. She'd fix up their small apartment, make it special. "Dum…dum…to waken with…" she sang softly.

Footsteps sounded in the hall. The door opened and her sister Edith stood there, apron tied around her waist, her face flushed from the heat of the kitchen. Her eyes sparkled, however, as she took charge.

"Mama sent me to help you. It's almost time." Edith walked to the closet where Rose's wedding dress hung on the door.

"Is Joe here yet?" Rose whispered, suddenly finding it difficult to speak.

Edith nodded. "The rabbi's here, too, and everyone's making their way upstairs now." She waved toward the front of the house. "We were smart to take all the beds apart and clear out the other rooms up here. There's lots more space than downstairs, especially now when it's too cold to use the back-yard."

Her sister kept chatting, but her hands were busy as usual. Edith was the oldest, their mother's first in line to assist and maybe the one most like Annie. A real *baleboosteh,* Edith could do anything, not that Rose and Gertie were left idle. In Annie Kaufman's house, everyone had jobs to do.

"Thank you, Edith." Rose reached for her sister. "So much cooking and cleaning…" Suddenly her eyes filled with tears, and Edith had a handkerchief ready to blot them.

"Bridal jitters? Don't worry, Rosie. I'm still your sister, and you're not going very far." Calm words filled with common sense. "I've enjoyed the cooking…I'm good at it. And…I recruited a lot of help."

"Well, the stuffed cabbage smells delicious," replied Rose, sniffing the faint, tangy aroma that wafted upstairs. Not that she had much appetite right then. And not that she hadn't helped prepare the sweet-and-sour dish. Goodness, they'd made vats of it this week and borrowed refrigerator space from the neighbors to store it.

"I've already arranged the gefilte fish and chopped liver on two big platters," said Edith. "Lots of crackers, challah and rye-bread squares. Every-thing's set to serve right after the ceremony, includ-ing the sandwiches."

At the last minute, Mama had ordered platters of deli sandwiches from the kosher caterer—an extravagance Rose hadn't expected. So yesterday, with her younger sister Gertie's help, Rose had prepared the potato salad and coleslaw to go along with the sandwiches. She'd been kept busy, but in the end, Mama and Edith were in charge of the wedding.

Edith reached for the dress and turned toward Rose. "It's time."

"Yes." Barely a whisper. *This is the beginning of the rest of my life.* Rose swallowed hard, then thought about Joe and felt a smile cross her face.

"It's not appropriate to walk down the aisle looking like the Cheshire cat," Edith said with a laugh.

Rose twirled in place. "But I'm happy, Edith. Wish me well."

"Of course I do, you goose. Now I wish you'd get into this dress!"

Rose removed her housecoat and raised her arms, allowing Edith to slip the ivory satin over her. A simple tea-length affair with three-quarter sleeves and empire waist, the dress showed off her curves. She'd spotted it in a secondhand store and it was three sizes too large for her. But she'd liked the style, knew the bias-cut skirt would flatter her, and bought it for twenty dollars. Then her work began. She took apart every seam, cut, pinned, basted and finally sewed it together again by hand stitch by tiny stitch, including the lace trim on the rounded neckline, lace that Edith had given to her.

"Slowly," said Edith now, motioning Rose to turn around. "It looks beautiful. Perfect. Wait— I'll roll the mirror to you."

"I'll go." Rose walked to the corner of the room and studied herself in the big, portable wood-framed mirror. Her thick, dark hair, styled with a pompadour and pulled back in a low chignon, was still neat. A light powder and a bit of rouge added color to her face. She reached for a pink lipstick and looked in the mirror again.

"A bride is supposed to look beautiful on her one special day," she whispered. "Maybe I do. At least a little."

"You *are* beautiful, Rosie!"

"As long as Joe thinks so," she said.

Edith's laughter rang out. "No problem there. The man's besotted. Let's get this veil on you."

"Wait a moment." Annie Kaufman's voice interrupted.

Rose's mother stood in the doorway, her husband right behind her. Only five feet tall and a hundred pounds, Annie filled any room simply by being "Mama." She swept toward her daughters, her keen eyes taking in the scene.

She spoke to Edith. "How is she?"

"Mama, I'm right here," said Rose.

"I know."

"She's fine," replied Edith. "Ready to walk down the aisle to Joe."

Now those sharp blue eyes studied Rose. "Is she

right, my Rosela? You're ready to stand under the chuppah and take your vows?"

"As long as Joe's waiting there for me," Rose whispered, "for the rest of my life."

Her mother nodded and kissed her on the cheek. "Good. Good. A good man is Joe." She walked back to Rose's father. "Shimon, do you have the gift?" she asked, using her husband's Yiddish name as she always did.

He reached into his pocket, and Annie returned to her daughter. "From your papa and mama, Rosela. Let's see how they look."

Rose opened the small box. Nestled inside were lovely pearl earrings. So unexpected. With shaky fingers, she put them on. Then her mama reached for the simple veil and, with a bobby pin, attached it to Rose's hair in the back. She gently pulled some of the netting down over her daughter's face, tweaked and fussed until it lay just so.

Annie Kaufman turned to her husband. "Shimon, tell the rabbi and Joseph that the bride is ready. It's time for a wedding!"

To: Joe Rabinowitz, 106th Infantry, U.S. Army;
somewhere in Europe
July 14, 1942

Dear Joe,
You left the States only last month, and I'm already trying to count the days until you come home. If we only knew when that will be!

Training with an artillery division is a step closer to the front lines. Please be careful! In my optimistic moments, I think the war will end quickly, before you have to fight. Of course, that's my heart speaking, not the army. But who knows? We have to have hope, no matter what.

I've decided that our six months together was our honeymoon. Maybe we've set a record for "longest honeymoon ever." I miss you so much and comfort myself with thoughts of our wedding and the time we had as man and wife.

I'm not sure how or when or if the army is forwarding mail, but I haven't received anything from you since you left. Maybe a letter will arrive this week. When it does, I'll save it in the beautiful keepsake box my sisters gave us as a wedding gift. I call it our Dream Box, Joe, because for now, dreams are all we have. I love you and miss you and will write to you every day.

Yours forever, Rose

August 15, 1942

Dear Joe,
A bunch of letters arrived today, and I read each one at least ten times. You describe everything so vividly. No wonder you became an English teacher! I will save the letters forever.

I have some news—news that will raise

*your spirits. My dear, darling Joe…I found out
today that you and I are going to be parents!
We have a baby "in the oven," as they say. So
now you have even more reason to take care
of yourself and be careful. I'm not surprised,
but I'm almost sorry you've been promoted
to sergeant even though the pay is better.
Casualty numbers are starting to be reported
here. Joe, I love you and I want you back.
Don't be a hero. Be a daddy instead.*

  Yours forever, Rose

"Hoo-ha!" Sergeant Joseph Rabinowitz sat on
his cot and leaned against the barn wall. His unit
was resting in the English countryside and these
quarters had served them well. A radio was playing
"If I Had a Talking Picture of You," and although
the sun's rays had long disappeared, he was able to
read by lamplight due to the working generators.

"What's up, Rabbi?" Almost everyone had a
nickname out here, and his was a term of affection—a short form of Rabinowitz. They called him
either Rabbi or Sarge. A bunch of swell guys.

Joe looked at his men, felt a grin cross his face,
then felt heat crawl up his neck. "For crying out
loud," he said to no one in particular. By now almost
every eye was on him, and he pushed himself
forward, his feet on the floor, and studied the fifty
faces turned toward him, half of them younger, half
of them older than his own twenty-eight.

He made his announcement: "Rosie says I'm going to be a daddy."

With those words, he realized he already was—army style. He choked on his own breath for a moment until the cheers broke out, and congratulations filled the air.

"Let's get this war over with so we can all go home and be daddies," said one of the men.

Exactly what Rosie wanted. "When we get back," said Joe, "every one of you is getting a cigar to celebrate my son."

"Or your daughter," a voice called out.

"Or my daughter," concurred Joe, looking at the speaker, the one guy in his platoon who came from the same neighborhood in Brooklyn as Joe—Charlie Shapiro. Joe hadn't known him before the war, but Charlie was an okay guy. Funny. Smart. Always thinking…but knew when to shut up, too—an excellent trait.

Joe glanced at his wristwatch. "Five minutes to lights-out. Can't use up all the juice."

The men settled in. By civilian standards, it was still early, but this was army life. A physical life with early reveille, even for the men on guard duty. With that thought, Joe took a flashlight and went outside to make his own rounds, have a word with the sentries.

All was in order and by the time he got back to his cot, the barn was quieter. The men, however, seemed restless. He could hear them toss and turn, still not ready for sleep. Which meant they'd start to think about home too much, about family, about being three thousand miles away from their familiar worlds.

"I didn't get any mail today," a voice said, confirming Joe's fears.

"And I got twelve letters all at once," said another.

Joe chimed in. "The same thing happens stateside, too. Rosie went a couple of weeks without anything, and I've been writing almost every day. The mail will get here…eventually." At least he could promise them that. Mail call was the highlight of the day, and he keenly felt their disappointment when men turned away empty-handed.

"Hey, Sarge," said Charlie. "Nobody's sleeping. How about finishing up the story of the Shrew, or the one about how you met Rosie."

"Again?" Joe chuckled. He really was a daddy telling bedtime stories. Shakespeare helped, and Joe knew every play—he'd have plenty of material to help his men get through this war. And as far as Rosie went…well, he could talk about her for hours.

He heard the others quiet down. As an avid reader, he thought the word *story* had a magic all its own. Here he was, in the middle of England, with a platoon of girl-starved soldiers who wanted to hear a story. It sounded crazy, but war was crazy, too.

"I'd never paid much attention to my sister's friends," he began, "until one day when Rosie dropped by to see Sarah. I'd answered the doorbell like I'd done a hundred times before, and there she was—dark, wavy hair with a curl on her cheek, and a smile so familiar to me, and yet, not familiar at all. I stared at her and couldn't say one single word. Not a sound. Then she looked up with her big brown eyes, and my heart took off like a…"

"…a racehorse at Aqueduct," chimed in Charlie.

Joe glanced at the soldier and laughed. Not very romantic, but…

"…and your heart took off like you'd never seen her before…" finished Eddie from Pennsylvania.

"That's right," Joe said softly, his laughter gone. "Like I'd never seen her before. And maybe I hadn't."

Twenty minutes later, most of the men had fallen or almost fallen asleep. Joe's eyelids felt heavy, too. He stretched out on the cot, and in moments, he was with his Rose.

> *To: Sergeant Joseph Rabinowitz, 106th*
> *Infantry, U.S. Army; Belgium, Europe*
> *January 21, 1943*
>
> *Dear Joe,*
> *Our beautiful daughter, Susan, was born yes-terday in a real hospital, not in the house. We are both fine. Mama is very happy to have a granddaughter named after her mother of blessed memory, Shifra, so thank you for agreeing. Your parents have already visited. Susan weighs six pounds, seven ounces and is a hungry little piggy, ready to nurse whenever I offer. I'm glad.*
>
> *My brother, Aaron, took a picture of me*

when I was big in the family way so you'd be able to see what I looked like, when you get home. God alone knows when that will be. My hopes rise and fall with every news report. The German defeat in Stalingrad last month sent my heart soaring again.

By the way, I did pay a visit to Charlie Shapiro's parents. Amazing that he lives in the area but neither of us knew him. His parents were happy to see me and eager to hear any news from the front. They are an older couple, and Charlie has no brothers or sisters. I could feel the stillness in their house, as though time has stopped and they are waiting. I saw the fear in their eyes. Maybe they could see the same in mine. I'll try to visit them again when the weather is better.

I'm tired now, but will write tomorrow and every day.

Yours forever, Rose

P.S. I'm giving baby Susan a kiss from you right now!

To: Sergeant Joseph Rabinowitz, 106th Infantry, U.S. Army; Belgium, Europe

June 5, 1943

Dearest Joe,

Last night Papa and Edith came to visit me at our apartment. When I opened the door and saw their faces, I knew something was wrong.

Mama is sick. The female-type cancer, and Papa asked if the baby and I could go back to live with the family. Everyone else has to go out to work, and Aaron's still in school. I hope you don't mind, but I have to take care of her.

I will put our belongings in boxes, and to tell the truth, there's not too much to pack. The money we get from the army I use for rent and food. Thank you for the extra coupons...

Rose paused in her writing to wipe her tears. Just a year and a half ago, she was the happiest woman in the world. Now her world had unraveled. Mama would not get better. She knew that simply by looking into Papa's eyes. Maybe Joe would die, too. She tiptoed to the baby's crib, leaned over and nuzzled her five-month-old daughter. Then she inhaled the distinctive fragrance of talc, shampoo and...baby.

"Sweet, sweet girl," she murmured. "You'll make your grandma smile, and maybe that will be the best medicine of all."

She glanced at the framed photo of Joe that Aaron had taken before Joe had shipped out. He was so handsome in his uniform. She and Susan started every day with a "Good morning, Daddy," and ended every evening with a good-night. When Joe returned, Susan would know her daddy.

Joe sighed and leaned against the wall of the foxhole, four feet beneath the surface. In his hand, he held a two-month-old letter from Rose that he'd received yesterday. It seemed his wife was fighting her own war on the home front. He prayed for her, his baby and his mother-in-law. He and Rose could find another place to live after he returned; in the meantime, however, his girls were better off surrounded by family. Certainly Annie Kaufman would be happy to play with her granddaughter regularly. In recent times, everyone focused on war casualties and yet death took its civilian toll, too.

He glanced around him, noting his men stretched out along the deep trench. Surely not as comfortable as a barn, but his troops didn't complain very much anymore. Their spirits were lighter since the day they'd made their pact.

His men had faced facts. In war, some would live and some would die. Joe's platoon had agreed that if one of them died, the survivors would contact the family of the fallen soldier and attest to his quick death on the battlefield. An instant ending. No pain and no suffering—regardless of the truth.

Joe didn't know who'd first voiced the idea, but he could picture the light that shone in the eyes of every man. He remembered the handshakes that clinched the deal and the spoken reminders before every military action since that time. The pact eased their hearts because, in the end, it would ease the hearts of the people they loved. And now every soldier kept a list of names and contact information with his belongings.

Maybe they'd all come out intact. Not likely, but who knew? Joe was optimistic again. It was summer now and much easier for the men to contend with heat rather than with the cold and snow. The North African campaign had gone well, and then an Allied armada had invaded Sicily last month on the ninth of July. Last week, Palermo fell to the Allies. He believed Italy's surrender would occur soon. One step closer to ending the war.

To: Sergeant Joseph Rabinowitz, 106th
Infantry, U.S. Army; France, Europe
December 7, 1943

Dear Joe,
Our second wedding anniversary is a sad time here. Mama was buried yesterday in cold, hard ground. I have no more tears left. But I think of you, and my heart fills up with love, so maybe love is stronger than grief. Please take care of yourself and come home safely. Susan will run to you—if she can stop falling down every time she tries to walk! Nothing stops her. You'd be so proud.

It's late but I can't sleep yet. A lot of people came to Mama's funeral, and of course, we are all sitting shivah. The house was filled with visitors last night and again tonight wanting to extend their condolences. I'm sure it will remain this way all week. You can tell Charlie Shapiro that his parents stopped by. I was sur-

*prised to see them since I've only visited twice.
I guess you and Charlie brought us together.
And of course, there's Susan. They fell in love
with her when they saw her last time.*

*On this street, black crepe hangs on two
front doors. I saw one dreaded army telegram
being delivered on a sunny afternoon when I
took Susan outside for some fresh air. I don't
ever want a telegram, Joe. Please take care
of yourself.*

Yours forever,
Rose

Cold. He was so cold, he and his men. The army
had issued boots and that helped, but living in a
foxhole was difficult in the winter. Two months ago,
Eisenhower had been named Commander of the
Allied Expeditionary Force in Europe, and Joe had
thought they'd move forward. But now, in February
of '44, even after a massive bombing campaign of
German aircraft factories, the enemy was still able
to produce weapons.

France was occupied, and Joe and his men were in
Belgium again, poised to go where most needed. He
wanted action. He wanted victory. He was not alone.

If only he could write Rosie a letter! He always
felt better getting his thoughts down on paper, sharing them with her, but his hands were too stiff from
the cold to hold a pen.

From a little way down the foxhole, he heard a

voice singing, "'If you knew Susie, like I know Susie…'" Someone else joined in and Joe smiled. Charlie Shapiro could sing, a real strong tenor. With a couple of others in the troop, he'd created an informal chorus. Great for when they had a twenty-four-hour stay at a rest camp, but while hugging a rifle in a trench?

Maybe the younger man was sticking it to the enemy—in his own style.

To: Sergeant Joseph Rabinowitz, 106th
Infantry, U.S. Army; Belgium, Europe
August 12, 1944

Dear Joe,
I hope you are able to get mail. After our boys'
massive landing on the French coast in June,
your letters have been a rare treat. I continue
to write each day, hoping some of the letters
will get through.

Your daughter is a pistol. She can even
raise a smile from her grandfather who has
not smiled since Mama got sick.

Susan's eyes have remained blue, and her
strawberry-blond hair curls in ringlets. When
she grins, this sweet dimple appears. More im-
portant, she says "Da Da" whenever she sees
your picture. Then she says, "Play!" and hits
the photo. Susan and I will be waiting outside
in front of the house when you return. You'll
come walking down the street as handsome as

ever, and we'll run to meet you, lightning quick,
before you get five steps from the corner. Can
you picture the scene like I can?

Until that day, I'll keep dreaming. And you
dream, too.

Yours forever,
Rosie and Susan

Joe folded the August twelfth letter he'd been rereading and put it in his back pocket. She'd have to
dream for both of them now. It was December 15,
1944. He was in new territory, the Ardennes Forest
on the Belgian-German border, and he had no time
for dreaming. He looked around at the heavily treed
woods. His was one of only three divisions holding
the area—a thin line for the area they patrolled. But
the staff commanders thought it wasn't a likely spot
for a German offensive.

Joe wasn't as concerned about fighting as he was
about the bitter cold. Snow was on the ground, flakes
in the air. Some of the locals had called it the snowiest
weather in memory, but he knew what to say to keep
his men alive overnight: "Keep moving. Stamp those
feet. Don't sleep, or you'll freeze your asses off."

His unit's heavy machine guns dotted the land.
Every troop also had a rifle. He was proud of them.
They'd worked together for a long time now, had
met combat in France and then returned to Belgium
where, last month, they'd had a twenty-four-hour
break at a rest camp. Oh, that had been fine. An easy

chair, soft lamps, warmth indoors—just to remind the men what civilization felt like.

Now they faced a chilly night in the Ardennes. What would tomorrow bring?

2007

In her Long Island bedroom, Rose reached into the Dream Box again. She unfolded a piece of paper and spread it out on the desk.

<u>WESTERN UNION</u>

FROM THE UNITED STATES DEPARTMENT
OF THE ARMY
*WE REGRET TO INFORM YOU
THAT YOUR HUSBAND
JOSEPH RABINOWITZ DIED IN THE
SERVICE TO HIS COUNTRY STOP
IN EUROPE THE ARDENNES STOP
SINCEREST CONDOLENCES*

She needed a cup of tea. Hot. Steaming hot. Gathering the Dream Box, the letters and the telegram, she carried them with her to the kitchen, placing them gently in the center of the table. Then she filled her ever-present kettle with water and turned on the gas stove.

Visiting the Dream Box usually exhausted her, so she hadn't made a habit of delving into it in recent years. It wasn't that her grief for Joe over-whelmed her anymore—her pang was for a young man she once knew, a fine man who'd died too soon, and that was the crux of her sadness. War heroes always died too young.

Would that be dear Matthew's fate, too? The possibility made her heart almost stop beating. Her arm trembled as she lifted the whistling kettle. Boiling water splashed on the counter when she started to pour.

"Rosie, be careful!" Charlie rushed to her side and eased the pot to the stove.

Startled, she glanced up. So lost in her thoughts, she hadn't even heard Paul and him come in.

Charlie glanced at the table. "The blast from the past almost did you in, Rosie."

She shrugged. "I'm fine. I can take it. But I'm glad you're here."

His eyes warmed, his smile widened. He kissed her. "I'm glad to be here."

There was a time, however, when her husband had hated the sight of the Dream Box, when it rep-resented everything wrong in their marriage. Thank God those days were over.

"Oh, Charlie," she cried, "I don't want Lizzy to go through what I did." She heard the anguish in her tone. The men heard it, too. Paul's complexion paled—Liz was his only daughter.

"Don't borrow trouble," Charlie said sharply, reaching for the telegram, handling it with a gentle touch. "We didn't know it at the time," he continued, "but it was the Battle of the Bulge, and we suffered the worst losses of the war."

"But thank God you survived," whispered Rose.

"God, alone, knows how." Charlie looked directly at her. "It was a December afternoon, and I was standing less than ten feet from Joe, aiming my machine gun at the enemy, shouting at my squad. We were fighting hard, but our division took the brunt of the counteroffensive, and—" he shook his head "—I heard him. I heard Joe giving orders, encouraging the men, and then...I glanced over and...I saw him take a hit. I saw him go down. His face...the surprise...but he died instantly. No pain. No suffering."

Rose patted his hand. "I know, Charlie. I know. You told me many times."

"And I'll never forget," he said softly. "I lost friends, my buddies." He paused, and Rose could hear his quick breaths. "I walked over five hundred miles after I was taken, and...and I saw things," he whispered, "no one should ever see."

Rose glanced at the table where she'd placed her and Joe's wedding invitation, her pearl earrings, the picture of her pregnant with Susan, a lock of Susan's hair in a glassine envelope, the folded letter Joe had placed in his pocket before he died and the army's teletyped message, still glued to the yellow paper it had been pasted on.

She tapped the telegram with her finger. "When

this arrived, I didn't hear the doorbell ring," she said. "But when Edith came upstairs to get me and could barely speak…I knew my life was over."

"Except it wasn't," declared Charlie in a strong voice. "Life goes on."

But she hadn't understood that. Not back then.

Chapter 3

June 30, 1945

Dear Joe,

A mistake! The army had made a mistake! After the telegram came, I received another V-Mail from you, and such radiant hope filled me, I couldn't breathe. Then I glimpsed the date of your letter...and collapsed. It had been written before you died. But for one crazy moment...

First Mama, and then you. I nursed Mama every single day, but she got sicker and sicker. I did everything the doctor suggested to keep her comfortable. I knew the end was coming, I really did, and yet when she died, I howled. My rock, my mama, was gone.

Then you died, and whatever hopes I'd retained for a good life disappeared like a cloud on a windy day. My world disappeared, and I did, too.

We hung black crepe on the front door after the telegram arrived. Your parents did the same. Then we held a memorial service without a burial. We sat shivah, of course, but I was like a puppet. It was as if someone else was moving my arms and legs so I could get through the days, one chore at a time. I cried whenever I looked at your picture, but Susan must know who her daddy is, so we said hello as always. I didn't know what else to do.

Papa was scared. After three months, he sent Susan and me to my uncle's farm upstate. Maybe I was having a breakdown. A change of scenery would help, he said. Edith and Gertie didn't protest, and I didn't care one way or another. I was still numb, barely going through the motions. The baby and I took the train, and my uncle met us at the station.

I planted seeds in his garden and watched them sprout. I saw calves being born. We collected hens' eggs and packed them for sale. Susan loved the freedom of the farm, the outdoors. We put her up on a pony, and she wasn't afraid.

Oh, Joe, Joe. You are missing so much! I need to tell you about Susan, about our lives, and I need to come to terms with you being gone—or at least try. Putting thoughts on paper is supposed to be therapeutic, but I want to communicate with a real person, a

*person I love and who loves...uh, loved...me.
I'm going to write to you, Joe, just like during the war.*

*Anyway, we stayed on the farm for almost
four months, until last week. I gained back a
little weight and am stronger now. I will never
be an innocent dreamer again. There are no
happily-ever-afters, but little by little, I will
put a life together for Susan and me. I'll try
not to let you down.*

Yours forever, Rosie

*P.S. Returning soldiers are everywhere now.
I see them in the streets, walking together
or with their girlfriends. My heart aches.
I struggle to smile and not look away.*

On July 4, 1945, after landing in New York
Harbor two weeks earlier, Charlie Shapiro lay
on his bed in the parlor of his parents' house in
Brooklyn, trying to absorb the fact that he was home.
That he'd returned alive and in one piece—for the
most part.

This front room had been converted to a bedroom, so he could look out at the street, at normalcy,
and on this Independence Day, at freedom. Flags
hung in every doorway.

His mother hovered over him, offering soup, soft
noodles, toast with jelly. She knew what to do to
heal his body, to help him regain fifty pounds and
his strength. His mind, however, was another matter.

He'd been in Europe for three years, but his memory bank seemed filled only by the Ardennes Forest and what came later.

Joe. Like a moving picture, Charlie could see his commander's face when he was flung backward. How his body had twisted toward Charlie—so darn close—but Charlie had to keep his machine gun firing at the enemy. There were too many enemy troops. The battle had raged for just over a month, but he'd been captured two days after Joe died and taken into the heart of Germany.

Four months later, after managing to survive the prison camp, after he'd been set free, when he thought he couldn't experience anything worse, he did. He watched inmates from liberated concentration camps die in front of him on the road. They were literally skin and bone, desperate for food, gobbling the army's candy bars only to die from dysentery. They'd endured much worse than he, and God alone knew how they'd remained alive that long. He'd never forget them.

Just like he'd never forget Joe. His sarge. The rabbi. Hell, he was everyone's rabbi regardless of background. Charlie wondered how Rosie was doing. She would have been notified months ago.

Tears trickled down the corners of his eyes and splashed on the pillow supporting him. His tears flowed too easily these days. Strange, when he hadn't shed one in captivity.

He heard his mother's footsteps.

"I made some fresh soup," she said. "Beef with barley. Not too much at once. See what you can do with this."

He'd never realized how hard eating could be, especially since he'd once lavished praise on everything his mother produced in her kitchen. The aromas still tantalized, but getting the food down wasn't easy.

He swallowed a spoonful. *Don't think. Bury the memories.* He looked into his mama's worried face. Took another spoonful. He could either eat or think, not both.

"I should visit Joe's wife," he said. "Joe would want me to check up on her." The pact. They'd shaken hands on it. A phone call or a letter wouldn't do here, not when Rose was only ten streets away.

He heard his mother's silence. Saw her stillness.

"Not yet," she said. "She just returned home, too."

"From where?"

His mother sighed. "Mr. Kaufman sent Rose and the baby to the country. To a farm upstate to rest. She's had a bad time. I wrote to you how she visited us—so nice of her to bring news of you—and, of course, we paid a shivah call when her mama died, but…after nursing her mother and then losing her husband… Even though she's back now, I don't know how strong she is."

Charlie shook his head. His mother's description didn't sound like the woman he'd heard about.

"Well, she has reason to feel despair," he began,

"but the way Joe talked, she could do anything, handle anything."

Tessie Shapiro's sad smile matched her eyes. "That was a man in love speaking, Charlie. Of course he thought his wife was one in a million."

Charlie said nothing. No point in arguing about something he couldn't prove, and maybe she was right.

"Could you fill the bowl again, Mama? I have to be able to walk ten blocks." If Rose needed some help, he'd be there—it was the least he could do for Joe's wife. Any of the guys would do the same.

A month later, on a warm Sunday evening in August 1945, Rose sat at the kitchen table, a paper tablet in front of her and a pencil in her hand. She was alone in the house except for Susan, who was asleep upstairs. Edith and Gertie had gone to Coney Island that morning for a day at the beach and hadn't returned yet. Her brother, Aaron, was out with some college friends, and her papa was visiting cousins a few blocks away.

Rose listened to the silence for a moment. Evening had crept up on her, its quiet taking her pleasantly by surprise. With that thought, her spirits lifted. For the first time in too long, she welcomed the task of planning a future for herself and Susan. A future without Joe. Her heart twisted each time she remembered he wouldn't be coming home, but she had to honor his memory. She had to raise their daughter in a healthy and happy way and do her best for a child who had never met her father. And never would.

Rose stared at the numbers on the paper in front of her—the monthly widows' and orphans' pension from the government. It was enough to contribute to the family household for now, but scarcely enough to pay a full rent for her own apartment as well as electricity, food, clothing for Susan and herself. Not unless Rose got a job. She had to think ahead. Be realistic. What if Papa died, too? Edith and Gertie had their own lives to lead. They'd given her so much support during the war, it was time to free them and show them she was fine.

She tapped the eraser on the table. Rearranged items in her budget. No question she needed a job, but with all the soldiers coming home and taking civilian jobs, who would hire her? And who would watch the baby? Maybe this was the right time to finish her college degree, just as she'd planned with Joe. Tuition was free and she was halfway through. If she loaded up on business courses, she could qualify for lots of jobs.

Sighing, she sat back in her chair. Maybe night school would work, she'd look into that possibility. And if Papa would babysit Susan—

The phone rang—two short rings, one long. Their signal on the party line. She answered it.

"This is Charlie Shapiro. May I speak with Rose Rabinowitz, please?"

Her heartbeat quickened. She knew that name—

Joe's friend from his unit. Dear God, Charlie was real. He'd come home.

She cleared her throat. "This...this is Rose."

"I don't know if you remember...but I served with Joe..."

"I know who you are," she whispered.

"Sorry," he said. "The phone has static. I couldn't hear you."

It wasn't the phone, it was her. She repeated the words loudly.

"Well, good," said Charlie. "Joe talked a lot about you and the baby...and I was wondering, since I live nearby...if maybe I could visit you. Maybe we could talk...if you have any questions...if you want to..."

Her mind swirled with indecision. Pros and cons. Sooners and laters. "Yes," she finally replied. "Yes, I think I'd like that." And if talking about Joe was too painful, she'd never have to see Charlie again.

Charlie Shapiro had light brown hair, hazel eyes and was as thin as a willow branch. He walked slowly, using a cane. He looked nothing like Joe.

"It's only temporary," he said, collapsing into a big wooden chair in the backyard. "If you think this is bad, you should have seen me a month ago!" He flashed a quick grin, and Rose realized he was trying to put her at ease even though she was technically the hostess.

"Maybe the walk was too much," she began.

Charlie shook his head. "I have to keep doing more. It's the only way to get totally well."

They sat in the shade of an oak tree, where Rose would be able to hear Susan cry through the bedroom window when she woke from her nap.

She asked if Charlie really wanted to talk about the war, about what he'd gone through.

"No," he replied, "but I wanted to meet you. To tell you that your Joe was a hero. A real hero to us guys in his unit."

She blinked at his sincerity. "Every one of you is a hero."

The man shook his head. "We were grunts. Joe was special. He kept us going when the going was rough."

And then Rose heard about the bedtime stories Joe told the men, about Shakespeare's tales and the celebrations when Susan was born. Joe had shared his family with his men, and they'd shared with him.

Charlie Shapiro was no slouch in the storytelling business, either; Rose could picture the scenes he recounted. He talked about Joe and assured her that his death came quickly and painlessly. She blinked tears away sometimes, she laughed sometimes. But all the while, her heart yearned…Joe, Joe, Joe.

She served Charlie sweetened tea and some plain sugar cookies she'd baked that morning.

"These are very good," he said with enthusiasm, downing his second cookie.

She wrapped a few in wax paper for him to take home. "If your mama wants the recipe, she can call me. You need to eat more."

She almost missed the flash of disappointment on his face, but she saw it and thought she understood. She'd made him feel less than a man.

"I'm sorry, Charlie. I shouldn't have said anything. And you're right—I didn't see you a month ago."

"No, I'm the one who's sorry, Rose. You're a swell girl, like Joe said. I'm just too sensitive these days. Guess it's time for me to go home."

"It's the war," she said briskly. "It's turned everybody upside down and inside out." She smiled at him. "You'll get stronger, Charlie. You'll be fine... Oh, did you hear that? Sounds as though Susan's up. Stay a moment longer and meet her."

Rose ran inside and up to the second floor, confident that Charlie would have settled back on his chair. She wasn't wrong. When she brought Susan outside five minutes later, he was waiting.

"Daddy?" The two-year-old pointed at Charlie.

"No, sweetheart." Rose cuddled her daughter, then looked at their guest. "She thinks every new man she sees is her daddy, especially if they're in uniform." She stood Susan on the ground.

Charlie looked down at himself. "Sorry. Nothing in my closet fits, and I haven't bought new clothes yet."

"Daddy," insisted Susan, walking to Charlie

and pulling at his hands. "Get up. Play wif me. Ple-e-e-as-e."

When Charlie laughed, his light eyes sparkled and crinkled up at the corners. He looked young. Goodness, he *was* young! Closer to Rose's age than to Joe's. She distracted Susan with a plastic pail and shovel. "Make a castle for Mr. Shapiro."

"Charlie," he said. "She can call me Charlie."

Rose glanced at him. "All right," she said slowly. "Make a castle for Charlie," she repeated to her daughter.

"Char-lie," said Susan, dimpling up at their visitor.

"Wowser! What a knockout. Just like her mother."

Damnation! Why had he made that last comment? He'd kick himself if he could. Now Rosie probably wouldn't want him to come around anymore.

He let himself in his front door and sniffed the air. His mom was cooking again. Too bad she had no other children to dote on. He walked into the kitchen and saw his dad was home, as well.

"I guess I'm later than I'd thought," said Charlie, putting the package of cookies on the counter. "From Rose," he explained. "They're delicious."

"Good. Good. You've got some color in your face, son. The walking was healthy." His dad examined him almost as closely as his mother did.

"I told him," said Tessie, "it's time to call his old friends. Start going around with young people again. He's too much alone in the house."

"So today I took your advice, Mama. I visited with a young person."

He'd been teasing, but his mother's eyes flashed before she closed them. When she opened them again, she looked calm. "You've done your duty, Charlie, so next time visit single girls. Not a grieving widow with a child, a woman who's still in love with her dead husband." She paused, and Charlie knew his mother well enough to know she'd done it purposely to heighten the drama.

"Do you understand what I'm saying?" she continued. "Rose Rabinowitz is not for you. She's not for anyone at this point—except Joe."

He eyed his mother. "You're worrying for nothing. I still have a way to go myself before any woman would want me, especially a wonderful woman like Rose."

Tessie turned to her husband. "Did you hear what he said, Sammy? I knew it! Talk to him. Talk to your son."

His dad winked at him. "Tessie, take a good look. Our boy seems better—he *is* better—since he came home. Praise be to God that he returned. Let him be happy." He rattled his newspaper. "Did you see these pictures, Charlie? Tessie? Look at this. Can you believe it?"

Almost every day another photo of a concentration camp was published in the paper. *Life* magazine had run a series on Buchenwald recently, and now the dailies were doing the same. The information had to get out, but it made Charlie sick.

"I don't have to see the pictures," he said, feeling himself tense up. "I saw the real thing." He fisted his hand and tapped it against his forehead. "And now the pictures are in here too much!"

He left the room and turned on the radio in the parlor before he sank onto his bed. Cole Porter's "Night and Day" filled the air. Now, *that* was a little tune he didn't mind having in his head. He closed his eyes and saw Rose.

October 12, 1945

Dear Joe,
Your friend Charlie has visited me several times since August. I don't know why really, except maybe he's lonely. He's gained some weight and is talking about going back to school on the GI Bill. In the meantime, he's got a job fixing cars.

He admired you, Joe. He told me more than once that all your men looked up to you and trusted you. "A born leader," he said, but what good is that talent now? Next time Charlie visits, I'm going to tell him to meet some other people. He needs to socialize with single people. Single women.

There's a marriage frenzy going on in America. The boys are home and most of the

girlfriends have waited. The singles are meet-
ing other singles. Edith met someone, too—a
real nice guy. You'll never guess where. On the
Boardwalk at Coney Island! His name is
Martin Schreiber, but we call him Marty. He
just got a job selling a line of costume jewelry.
I think he'll do well—he's friendly and talka-
tive. He was a cook during the war, in North
Africa and Europe, but he never talks about
that. Funny how the newspapers talk but the
soldiers don't.

Your mama says that Susan is growing by
inches between every visit, and I agree. Our
daughter chatters nonstop now—in two lan-
guages! She says her prayers with Papa in
Yiddish, and sings songs with him in Yiddish,
too. Charlie sings along with them some-
times. What a beautiful voice he has, but I bet
you know that already.

Oh, I forgot to mention about Gertie. She's
going to be a cop. That's right, a police-
woman. She applied to be in the first female
class trained as New York City police officers.
Isn't that something?

That's about all for now. I love you, Joe.
Always will.

Yours forever, Rosie

Rose folded the letter and added it to her collec-
tion in the Dream Box. She had so many now, the

box was filling up. She'd have to store them some-where else soon.

She thought about what she'd written. Everyone was moving on in some way. Marriage. Jobs. A future. Everyone except her. If only Joe had come home. She kept his letters from the front, safe in a folder underneath her nightgowns. Her mouth tight-ened before she chuckled. Nightgowns. Now, what did that signify?

She didn't have to be Sigmund Freud to figure it out. She missed the intimacy, the cuddling, the love-making. The nights were long, lonely times. She never mentioned it to anyone, not even to Edith, whom she trusted. It wasn't right to talk aloud about such private thoughts, but the truth was that she'd known exquisite love and tenderness in the marriage bed, and of course, had held out for the promise of Joe's return. And now what?

The only answer she had was to forget about it and concentrate on real problems: a job, an educa-tion, a future for her and Susan. Someday she had to be able to totally support herself and her daughter.

Rose reached for the City University schedule she'd picked up at the library. Night classes for next term. If Papa babysat two evenings a week, she'd go to the business college on Twenty-third Street. If she couldn't earn money right now, at least she'd be doing *something* to secure a future. And when Susan was old enough to go to school, Rose could go to work.

* * *

"Papa won't do it," said Rose a week later, pushing Susan's carriage toward Bedford Avenue, Charlie walking alongside her. "Says he doesn't want me out alone at night riding the subways. I just don't understand him. The trains are safe, and all his other children have college diplomas. Does he think I'm a dummy?"

Charlie had never seen Rose worked up before. Her cheeks were pink, partly from the cooler weather, partly from her frustration. Her dark eyes sparkled, and her long hair bounced in thick, springy curls as she walked swiftly down the block. It was a Sunday afternoon at the end of October, and when he'd shown up to visit, Rose suggested taking a walk.

To his pleasant surprise, he'd kept up with her, but was afraid she'd bump into the other pedestrians if she continued her crazy pace. "Slow down, Rose, would you?" he asked.

She turned to him, and more color filled her cheeks. "Oh, I'm so sorry, Charlie. I forgot."

"No, no. I'm fine," he reassured. "It's them I'm concerned about." He motioned toward the others out for a stroll. "You're a dangerous woman with a weapon."

Her smile delighted him, set his heart pounding. He couldn't hide the truth from himself anymore, no matter what story he told his mother. He was in love with Rose. Had been halfway in love with her just listening to Joe's bedtime stories. But after he'd met her and spent time with her...he had no doubt at all. Except she still loved Joe.

"Here's an idea for you," said Charlie. "Tell your papa that you won't be traveling alone. I'll take classes, too, and we can go together."

If her eyes opened any wider, they'd fall out of her head.

"Really?" she almost squealed. "You'd sign up on the same night? Charlie! That's wonderful. Thank you. Thanks so much...but wait a minute. Do they teach auto mechanics at City College?"

"Nope," he replied, liking that she was thinking about him. "But someday I'll own my own shop, and I'll need to know how to run a business. I dropped out of college before the war to bring some money into the house. My dad—he was giving everybody credit in his grocery store. I asked him how he expected to make a living..." Charlie chuckled and shook his head. "He never answered me. But now, why not go back to school?"

"No reason," said Rose, "as long as you're up to it. I mean, you're working during the day, too. Can you do both?"

"It'll be good for me," he said. "Keep me busy." Keep his mind occupied is what he meant. The more he had to distract him, the better off he was. Maybe his bad memories would fade...

"Well, this is turning out to be a better day than I'd

thought," said Rose. "You're a good friend, Charlie, doing me a big favor. Maybe I can do one for you."

"I'm fine. Don't need any favors…unless you're baking those cookies again."

Her delighted laugh made him want to laugh, too. Did she have any idea how beautiful she was? How adorable?

"Anytime, Charlie. I'll bake them anytime at all. I wasn't thinking about cookies, but about introducing you to some of my girlfriends. You're a nice guy, Charlie. You should meet someone."

I already have. But of course, he kept his mouth shut. "I don't think so, Rosie. I'm not ready."

At her look of disappointment, he added, "But if I change my mind, I'll let you know. How's that for a bargain?"

"I'll hold you to it." She peered at him from under her lashes. "Of course, if you wait too long all the women might be taken. So, do you want to change your mind now?"

He had to laugh. "Nope. I'm happy just the way I am."

At that moment, an older woman strolled by and peeped in the carriage at Susan. "What an adorable little girl you have. How lucky for you." She beamed up at Rose and Charlie.

"Uh…" began Rose.

"Thank you," said Charlie. "We think so, too. Very lucky, indeed."

"Bye, little sweetheart." The woman waved as she moved on.

Rose stared at him. "She thought…uh…that we…"

Charlie grinned, loved seeing her rattled, especially in the direction he wanted her to go. "She sure did think so."

Rose glanced at him, at Susan, at the woman's retreating back. Once more she focused on him, her expression concerned. "That isn't right."

He shrugged. "Why? We don't know her. So who is it hurting?"

"Life isn't a game, Charlie, and I'm afraid that in the end, it will hurt you."

He understood what she was saying—very clearly—and he looked her straight in the eye. "I'm willing to take my chances."

Chapter 4

January 20, 1946

Dear Joe,

We celebrated Susan's third birthday today. Your parents came with Sarah, and Edith's fiancé, Marty, took lots of pictures. Susan caught on very quickly and smiled each time the camera focused on her. A little Shirley Temple! I will give your mama some of the pictures.

Charlie came to the party, too. He brought her a jack-in-the-box, which makes Susan giggle uproariously. Of course, she plays with it ten times in a row the way small children like to do, but it gives her mama a headache.

Papa seems tired these days. He moves slowly. Of course, he's not been the same since Mama passed away. We all miss her terribly, but somehow our lives continue. Next month Edith and Marty will get married in a lovely restaurant with a private party room in the back. Gertie and I will help decorate the chuppah with colorful ribbon, and the rabbi will perform the wedding service right there. I'm so happy for Edith. More important, she and Marty are a very loving couple. They've already put a rental deposit on an apartment on Ocean Avenue. It's a nice neighborhood, but not within walking distance.

Yours forever,
Rose

Rose had managed to register at City College for an accounting course that met on Tuesday nights. Charlie had classes on both Tuesday and Wednesday nights.

"Next semester, I'll sign up earlier," said Rose as she and Charlie walked from the train station toward her house one March evening a month after Edith's wedding. "It will take me forever to get my degree at this rate."

"Not your fault, Rosie. Your father didn't offer to babysit until the last minute. And with Gertie's crazy schedule…"

"I know," she replied. "And at least it's not because he doesn't want me to go to school. Papa says education is the key to the future."

"He means it's the way out of poverty," said Charlie.

"I'm doing the best I can," she sighed. She

mended her dresses and made Susan's clothes out of any scrap material she could find. On occasion, she bought a yard of corduroy and cut pants and a pinafore from it, allowing big hems which she'd let down as Susan grew.

Everyone had learned how to stretch a penny during the depression and then during the war. Old habits were hard to break. Even though the economy now looked promising, Rosie's own future didn't. At least, not yet. She couldn't afford to lose her thrifty ways.

They'd reached her brownstone, and Charlie walked her up the outside flight of stairs to the main entrance. She turned the key in the lock and swung the door open. "Thanks, Charlie."

Susan's cries echoed through the hall. "*Zayde, my zayde*... No *shluffen*...don't sleep...wake up!

"Papa!" Rose ran down the corridor to the back bedroom, hearing Charlie's footsteps behind her. Her father lay faceup on Rose's bed. The baby sat on top of him, crying and calling for her grandpa, hitting his chest with her little hands.

"Oh my God," gasped Rose. "No...no...no...!"

Then Charlie was there, lifting Susan, putting her into Rose's arms. Putting his ear to her father's chest. Listening and feeling for the pulse in his neck. Did he learn that in the army? Crazy world. He motioned her out of the room with Susan, who still made too much noise, but she stood in the doorway, and when Charlie finally looked at her and shook his head, she knew.

"I'm so very sorry," said Charlie. "He's gone." He stepped toward her, his arm outstretched, but she put up her hand.

"No," she said again, her voice hoarse. "He can't be." She handed Susan to Charlie, ran downstairs to the kitchen and called the doctor. Cold seeped through her body; she started to shiver. And there was Charlie again, one arm carrying Susan, the other around Rose. They climbed back up to the bedroom.

"Hang on, Rosie," he whispered. "I won't leave you."

She took a deep breath and nodded, then heard the rap at the door. The doctor moved quickly, but within minutes she knew the Kaufman children had another funeral to plan. Annie and Shimon were together again.

"I came home too late," she whispered. "Too late. What happened to him? I shouldn't have gone to school."

The doctor shook his head. "His high blood pressure, Rose…" he said. "Your being in school made no difference. In my opinion, he had a massive stroke. But if you want an autopsy done…?"

"No, no. He wouldn't want that. Why didn't he tell me his blood pressure was so high?"

"That I don't know, my dear, but I do know the outcome would be the same whether you knew or not. Unfortunately, medicine doesn't have all the answers yet."

One by one, her siblings came home. Somehow Charlie had reached them all. Even Gertie, who was on the four-to-midnight shift at the women's jail in Manhattan, managed to return to Brooklyn. Aaron had been about to leave his girlfriend's house not far away. Edith and Marty had taken a taxi, and Susan had been given some milk and was now sleeping again—thanks to Charlie's patience with her.

Within an hour, Rose was surrounded by her family. She looked at the circle of sad faces. "Can adults be orphans?" she whispered. "No one stands between us and heaven anymore."

"We have each other," replied Edith. "We're a family and always will be."

"You have friends, too," said Charlie, his eyes going from one Kaufman sibling to the other before looking directly at Rose. "You can count on me for anything at any time. Always. No matter what the circumstances."

She heard his promise. A promise given because he was Joe's loyal friend who'd thrived on Joe's family stories when they were both a long way from home. Maybe every man in the unit fell a little bit in love with Joe's wife. Poor Charlie happened to live close enough to meet her.

Her brother stood up and began to chant the mourner's prayer, the Kaddish. Automatically, Rose and her sisters joined in, but it was Charlie's voice she heard. Charlie's beautiful, strong tenor.

* * *

Two weeks after her father's funeral, on a Sunday morning in late March, Rose called a family meeting in the house on Hewes Street. Pale sunlight filtered through the kitchen curtains illuminating the dust motes dancing in the air. Rose poured coffee from a freshly brewed pot and was proud of her steady hand—no spills. She'd baked cookies and a challah, which had risen beautifully, and set them out with cheeses and herring. Aaron had gotten a rye bread and bagels from the bakery.

Susan lay in Edith's arms, drinking from a bottle. Since the night her *zayde* died, Susan had refused to use a glass and insisted, in a loud voice, in using a bottle. Rose didn't have the heart to say no, especially when her daughter had also begun wetting her bed again after being dry for months. Who knew what memories she'd stored in her head about that awful night? If she needed the comfort of her bottle, so be it.

Now Rose studied the group of drawn faces around her, in mourning for their father and also needing what could be a painful discussion about the future. About the house. Rose returned the coffeepot to the stove, took her seat and plunged in.

"This house was left to all of us, but within six months, only Susan and I will be living here. Is that right?" She looked at Aaron, who nodded, and Gertie, who did likewise.

"Maddy and I are planning to get married this summer," said Aaron. He turned to Edith. "Should I postpone…because of Papa? Wait until a full year passes?"

Rose had her own opinion, but was curious as to what Edith would say. Her sister produced a sad smile. "Frankly I think this family has been through enough tragedy recently. Life must continue. Papa liked Madeline very much, so I think a quiet affair would be appropriate. But you're still young, Aaron. Only what? Twenty-two? You and Maddy can wait if you like."

But Rose saw what Edith didn't—Aaron's dark brown eyes reflected a maturity beyond his years. As she watched, he moved his head slowly from side to side, the planes of his face tense, his mouth tight before he spoke.

"Young, Edith? I haven't been young since I was eight or nine. Or before then. Do you think it was easy being the only son and the youngest child? I never wanted to disappoint him. And then one, two, three—we lost Mama and Joe and Papa. I lost my best friend, Georgie, in the war, and he was just a year older than me. Young? No, Edith. I'm not feeling very young."

He paused, but Rose sensed he had more to say and she waited. "But I do feel—" Aaron continued slowly "—lighter when I'm with Maddy. Like a weight's been lifted. Maybe, just maybe, that's what happiness is supposed to feel like."

"Then get married," ordered Rose, jumping to her feet. "We are still alive!"

The statement reverberated through the room, and suddenly all eyes were on her. Her cheeks burned to the tips of her ears. She had no idea where her thoughts had come from—or that she believed them.

"Attagirl, Rosie! That's the sister I used to know," called out Gertie. "*Mazel tov.* So, are you back among the living now? Should I thank Charlie Shapiro?"

"What do you mean 'among the living'?" asked Rose. "I live up to my responsibilities every day."

"Gertie!" Edith's reproving voice. "Stop it. Keep a civil tongue in your head."

"I'm just saying—"

"Well, don't say. We have other things to discuss."

Irreverent Gertie. A soft heart, a sense of humor, but not afraid of stepping on toes sometimes. Maybe becoming a cop was a good decision.

"Our tenants on the third floor want to buy the house," said Rose, eager to focus attention away from personal issues. "I told them we weren't ready to decide yet. But even if we did, we'd need at least six months." She glanced at Aaron. "I took your wedding into account."

Then she looked at Gertie. "And you want to share an apartment with some of your policewomen friends, right?"

Gertie nodded. "I'm assigned in Manhattan. I'll be closer to work and, frankly, I'll have a better social life."

With those words, everyone chuckled. "Gertie," said Rose, "no one has a better social life than you. I've watched you go out time and again with a different guy, and then, *poof!* It's over in a week."

Now it was Gertie who blushed. "Well, that's not the same as a good social life."

Rose stared at her little sister. Bright, sharp, articulate, but not at the moment. "Maybe it's not a *busy* social life you're after," said Rose. "Maybe you want a dependable one. Just one good man. The right man for you."

For once in her life, Gertie did keep her tongue still. Surprised, Rose glanced at her older sister. Edith nodded. Rose had hit a nerve.

"Back to the house," said Rose, changing the subject for Gertie's sake. She turned toward Aaron. "Do you think you and Maddy might want to live here? The house is big enough for both of us."

Her brother squirmed in his chair, then stared at her. "Maybe...maybe we all need new beginnings. Because of the housing shortage, construction is booming all over the city. Brand-new apartment buildings are going up along the Belt Parkway. Maddy's already looked at them. She said other people—many young couples—were inquiring the same day."

Rose understood exactly what he was telling her. New beginnings for a new couple. The way it should be. Hadn't she loved setting up the apartment she and Joe had rented? "It's okay, Aaron. Not to worry."

She stared at each person she loved. "So it's settled. We sell the house to Mr. and Mrs. Levy in about six months."

"But what about you, Rose? Where will you go?" asked Gertie. "Maybe you can become *their* tenant," she continued, answering her own question. "Just make a switch with them, and you don't have to worry about repairs or paying bills or anything to do with the house."

Rose didn't understand immediately why her sister's suggestion caused her to choke but it did. She coughed, then she inhaled, and her words gushed like the sea pouring through a broken dyke.

"So instead of worrying about the house," she began, "I'll watch Susan look for her *zayde* every hour. I'll watch her run down to the second floor searching for her unca Aaron and tante Gertie, and then want to go in the backyard—which won't be ours—to play on her swing or to dig with her shovel." Her nails bit into her palms.

"I've lost my Joe," she said, "which is bad enough, but soon, every time I walk through the front door, I'll be looking for you, too. But none of you will be here. Staying here would be like living with the ghosts of my family." Swaying slightly, she grabbed the back of her chair. "I can't do it," she said, her breath coming in gasps. "I can't live with ghosts. I have to move. Like Aaron said, new beginnings."

No one spoke. The air seemed to reverberate with the silence. Until… "You should get married again."

Startled, Rose glanced at Gertie. "No. That won't happen. Joe may be gone, but he's still here." She tapped her chest.

"I'll find out the exact rent of the new apartments," said Aaron. "Maybe when we sell the house, you could get one in the same building with Maddy and me."

She smiled at her sweet brother. "Thanks, Aaron. But after we pay off the mortgage and divide the sale price by four, we'll each come out with bubkes. Peanuts! Peanuts won't last long, and then I'd be back to where I started. Better to use the money as a cushion for emergencies."

She looked at each face, which was filled with concern. "What I really need is a good job to supplement the war pension. And to get a good job, I need to finish college. So all of you are going to help me…by babysitting."

She felt them relax a bit although a furrow still sat on Edith's forehead. "In the meantime," said her sister, "don't burn your bridges. We still haven't solved your living problems. Aaron should inquire about rentals, and you'll tell the Levys we'll sell in six months—after his wedding—but that you get first dibs on the third-floor apartment…just in case. We'll try to figure out something else by then."

Rose nodded.

* * *

On a Sunday evening a month later, Charlie whistled cheerfully as he walked down the street toward his house. A spring afternoon with Rose and the baby always put him in a good mood. Today they'd gone to Prospect Park and let Susan fly on the "big girl" swings. He'd watched Rose as she'd watched her daughter, noticing how delighted she was every time Susan had giggled. He'd watched her stroke the child's pink cheek.

"This has been a wonderful afternoon," she'd said later. "Thank you, Charlie."

"You needed to rest your eyes from all the mending," he'd said.

"I rested yesterday, on *Shabbos*. I don't work on Saturday, so I'm cheating this afternoon by taking another free day."

Rosie had created a job for herself. After the meeting with her family, she'd decided to take in other people's mending and also sew new clothes. She'd explained it to him the way she'd explained it to her sisters.

"I can sew in the house. Even with the men home from the front, some women have continued to work, so they don't have time for the mending. As for the women who are at home…well, I'm a good stitcher. I'm not afraid of competition."

Rose hadn't dawdled. She'd gone from idea to reality in a week. She'd spread the word in the neighborhood with the "most friendly women who knew everyone"—the busybodies. But when

Charlie had joked about it, Rose had remained silent. Only her eyes had twinkled. Shortly afterward, she'd had a stroke of luck obtaining contract work through a manufacturer's rep in the garment center. Actually, it was more than luck. Charlie had repaired the car of the rep and told him about Rose, and that man had told someone who told the right person to contact her.

Rose. Rose. Rose. She sat in the back of his mind seven days a week. And now that he'd regained his full health after nine months at home, the nights were as hard as he often was.

He let himself into the house through the street-level door and could hear his parents' voices as he made his way toward the kitchen in the back.

"He's in love with her, Tessie. So get used to it."

"I can't. He should have his own family, not a widow with a child."

Charlie halted in the shadow of the kitchen door.

"But she's a nice girl," replied his father.

"So what? There are lots of nice girls in New York. The point is that she's Joe's wife—Charlie's commanding officer. That's what this is all about."

"Do you know something I don't, Tessie? Did Joe ask Charlie to watch out for her...and now Charlie feels responsible? I'll talk to him. A man doesn't sacrifice his personal life out of obligation—not in today's new world anyway."

"I don't know anything special, but do you see him courting anyone else?" asked Tessie. "He doesn't even realize what he's doing—courting her through her daughter… He brings Rose lamb chops. Would any mother turn down lamb chops for her child? Of course not. Rose Kaufman—I mean Rabinowitz—is not stupid, but she's a poor woman, and Charlie has a good job at the Texaco fixing all those cars. She'll take from him. Mark my words, she'll break his heart."

Charlie stepped into the room. "That's enough! Both of you. If you have something to say, tell me. If you have questions, you ask me. Don't talk about Rose behind her back."

His mother didn't miss a beat. "I have a question."

He nodded.

"Does *she* love *you?*"

Staring into his mother's eyes, he replied, "I don't know about love. I know about trust. She trusts me."

Unbelievably, he saw tears well in her eyes.

"Charlie, Charlie…after all you've been through, you deserve the fairy tale, the excitement, the falling in love. A nice wedding. Like our friends' children are having. We want to see you happy."

"Then you've got what you want," said Charlie. "Being with Rose makes me happy." He turned from them. "I'm going for a walk. Don't hold supper for me." He left the house and allowed the door to slam behind him.

After the conversation with his parents, Charlie decided to change his tactics with Rose. He brought flowers. A newly minted penny for good luck. A shiny gold thimble to protect her finger when sewing. And sharp scissors, too. He wanted to take her dancing, but Rose was in mourning for her father. Instead, he contented himself with her company as they continued their college classes midweek and his visits on Sunday afternoons.

Sometimes she invited him to the house on a Saturday night if Edith and Marty visited, or if Aaron and Maddy were going to be home. They played gin rummy, drank coffee and talked about their lives, about the country, about Hitler. About an article just published in the Netherlands detailing the discovery of a young girl's diary.

He knew about the plan to sell Rose's house. He knew she was working too hard for the money she earned—she'd joked about needing eyeglasses soon—and it tore him up to see her hopeful smile and hear her talk about the next week's possible earnings. Her compensation fluctuated according to the demand for piecework. If his heart were any fuller with love for her, it would burst. He'd been visiting Rose for almost a full year, had gone through tough family issues with her. It was time to take a stand.

One Saturday evening in late June, while Aaron and Maddy were home and able to watch Susan, he invited Rose to go for a walk with him—alone. He ignored Aaron's raised brow, his tiny smile. Charlie was too nervous to do anything else. Everything was at risk. If she turned him down, not only his hopes but their friendship would dissipate, as well. A burned suitor did not remain in the picture—at least, *he* could not.

He couldn't live without hope, but he also couldn't live with false hope. Not any longer.

"Look at that gorgeous moon," said Rose as soon as they were outside. Her voice echoed her pleasure at the sight of the full moon so luminous in the clear sky.

"I'd rather look at the gorgeous girl standing next to me," said Charlie softly.

"The…the…what?" Rose tilted her head back and studied him. He didn't flinch.

"You heard me, Rose," he replied, taking her hand and leading her away from the house. "You're the prettiest girl I've ever known. You're smart and clever and wonderful. I've admired you from the first time I met you."

She didn't say anything, and for a moment he wasn't sure she'd ever respond. But then she did. "And you've been a wonderful friend, Charlie. Someone I can talk to about almost anything… about anyone…including Joe."

She couldn't have been clearer about her feelings. About where she stood—and he stood. But his D-day had arrived.

"Are you going to mourn Joe for the rest of your life?" he pursued. "Do you want to be alone forever?"

She pulled away from him. "Why are you asking me these questions? Why do you care what I do? You're confusing me."

A breakthrough. He stepped in front of her, and she was forced to look up at him. "The answer to each question is the same, Rosie. I love you. It's as simple as that. I've loved you for a long time, and right now my heart's beating faster than a bass drum because I've said the words out loud." He reached for her hand and brought it to his chest. "Can you feel it?"

They had paused beneath a streetlamp at the corner. Her fingers were splayed across his left side. He saw her nod, heard her whisper, "Yes. Yes, I can feel it racing."

"I would be honored, Rose, if you would marry me. I would be honored to be your husband. Let's you and I make a life together—and give Susan a daddy."

He felt her flinch and hardened his tone before she could respond. "Joe's not coming back, Rose," he said. "For God's sake, Susan's never even met him!"

She stepped back, and he saw tears trickle down her cheeks. "I know that, Charlie. Believe me, I know that. But marrying you is not fair. Not fair to *you*."

His heart started to sing. "I'll take that chance."

"But Joe was my *bershert*," she protested, allowing her tears to fall harder. "My soul mate. The one who was meant to be. And *your* soul mate is still out there." She waved her arm at the night.

"Shh…" he whispered, putting his finger gently over her lips, and slowly bending toward her until his mouth touched hers. He heard her quick intake of breath, but she remained with him, allowing the kiss to deepen, allowing herself to relax. And when she stepped away a moment later, he didn't protest until he saw that her eyes were as big as the moon above them. Until he heard her first words.

"What have I done?" She placed her hand over her mouth.

"You've rejoined the human race," he said. "And you're not hiding away again." He leaned toward her, gently moved her hand and kissed her once more.

Long Island, 2007

"Are you planning to tell the entire cockamamie story tomorrow night?" asked Charlie, gathering the keepsakes his wife had pulled from the Dream Box. "I might not show up if you do!"

Rose patted his hand and reached for her report card from City College. She'd earned an A in that accounting class. "Not to worry," she said. "I have something else planned for the party."

"Oy vey. What?"

Rose shook her head. "Trust me. You'll like it."

Paul laughed. "Dad doesn't look convinced."

"I know my wife," replied Charlie. "She can still surprise me."

"Why thank you, Charlie," said a smiling Rose. "I consider that a beautiful compliment."

Her husband blushed, and she loved it, but took pity on him by changing the subject.

"Here's Edith and Marty's wedding invitation, may they rest in peace." The paper stock had yellowed, but the words were as clear as the day they had been printed.

"And there's the invitation for my brother's wedding." She looked at Paul. "But Charlie and I didn't have any invitations."

"Why not?"

"Because only a few people came. Not very festive, I'm afraid. I remember, I wore a dark blue suit...with a fitted jacket..."

"She looked beautiful in that suit and a little hat with a thin netting. I couldn't take my eyes off her..."

"We went to the rabbi's study in the synagogue with just my sisters and brother, their spouses and Papa Charlie's parents..."

"Don't forget Susan..."

"Susan, too. And afterward, we went to a little dairy restaurant on Bedford Avenue. As weddings go, it was a nonstarter."

"You got robbed, Charlie," said Paul.

"Nope," Charlie replied. "I won the prize. I won my Rose, but she came with a bunch of thorns. So if you think we sailed merrily into a happily-ever-after, you'd have to think again. Not for twenty-five more years."

He reached for Rose's hand, but looked at his son-in-law. "Our Lizzy and her Matthew—they have a lot ahead of them. A lot to learn. This life we've been given...they need to know that it's all about the journey. The wonderful, terrible and amazing journey."

"But they don't need to know about *our* journey," insisted Rose.

"I agree," said Charlie, while Paul remained quiet. The ensuing silence was broken by the sound of the front door opening and a familiar voice calling out, "Hello, everybody."

Rose swiveled in her seat. "In the kitchen, Susan. Come join the preparty party."

"Any coffee left?"

Rose watched her eldest child drop kisses on her dad's and husband's cheeks as she made her way to the stove. Taller than her mother, even in Rose's prime, Susan, at sixty-three, still walked with erect posture, her chin forward as if she was in a hurry. The strawberry blonde of her youth had darkened to brown, which had since evolved to a uniform steel gray, straight and casual to her shoulders. Not every woman could carry that shade, but Susan could, and when she followed Rose's wardrobe advice about color and style, the results were stunning. Of course, her daughter didn't always take Rose's advice…not now and not in the earlier years. But they didn't do too badly together.

Susan set her cup on the table and sat down. "This is cozy," she said, "especially the trip down memory lane." She nodded toward the Dream Box. "But I'm not in the mood."

"Oh, no, here we go again," groaned Paul. "She's upset that Matthew won't allow us to repay his government education loans. She's upset that Lizzy won't talk him into it."

"Matt's his own man," began Charlie.

"He's got a responsibility to his wife," retorted Susan. "His pregnant wife. My daughter. Your granddaughter." She glanced at Rose. "Do you want her to be a widow before she can really be a wife? The baby might not know its father, just as I didn't know mine."

Rose saw the flash of pain cross Charlie's face. "That's not fair, Susan!" she protested. "*This* dad treated you better than he did your brother and sister. In fact, how many dads would have let you spend their wedding night with them?"

Susan jumped from her seat and ran to Charlie. "I'm so sorry, Dad. I didn't mean it personally... I'm just jumpy about Liz and Matt."

And then, as though Rose's words had just registered, she turned to her and asked, "What are you talking about, Mom? What wedding night?"

Chapter 5

"What wedding night?" repeated Rose, before pointing at Charlie and then at herself. "Our wedding night." She sighed. "All I was aiming for in those days was a college diploma. Instead, I got a marriage license and everything turned out fine anyway."

"Ha! It only worked because she wound up with both," said Charlie. "Your mother wanted that degree so much, a degree like her sisters and brother had. But it took her a while to earn it—to graduate and establish her career—because after we got married came the business of making a life together."

Starting with the wedding night. Rose, the octogenarian, could feel herself blush at the memory…

She hadn't given the "afterward" much thought—after the wedding ceremony. After the luncheon. After everyone wished them a final *mazel tov* and went to their own homes. She hadn't planned to have Susan with them that Sunday evening until her daughter refused to go home with Tessie and Sam. At almost four years old, Susan knew what she wanted. "Daddy!"

Charlie melted as he always did with the child who had taken to him from the first time they'd met. He had a way with people, Rose had learned— young and old—and Susan was no exception. She supposed she wasn't, either. The man had a good heart, and somehow she'd actually married him.

So she, Charlie and Susan made their way to the apartment they'd rented near Aaron and Maddy's, right after the brownstone on Hewes Street had been sold.

They rode the elevator to the fifth floor and walked to apartment 5F. Charlie turned the key, pushed the door wide and looked at her with shining eyes. "Welcome home, sweetheart."

Before she could protest, he'd swept her into his arms and crossed over the threshold into the foyer. Then he twirled her while she held on tight. When he slowed down, he kissed her cheek and, little by little, lowered her until she was standing next to him. His arms remained around her as he leaned closer, touching his lips to hers.

She inhaled the fragrances of soap and Old Spice and man, tinged with a trace of celebratory schnapps. Familiar aromas. His hands felt sure and strong, his mouth firm on hers. She shivered. Her breath shortened. The intimate part of marriage had been so good. If only Joe— She stopped herself and looked up.

It was Charlie's green eyes that gazed back at her, eyes now darkened with desire, and it was Charlie's lips that caressed her own. Her body had responded. *She* had responded. So what did that mean? She stepped away from her new husband, confused.

He studied her, then said softly, "If I dwelled on the past, I'd have to be locked away in one of those mental institutions. I love you, Rose. Whatever else might be on your mind right now, remember that. Please."

She couldn't speak, so she nodded. The man knew she'd been thinking of Joe, but it was better not to put it into words—especially on their wedding night.

"You're a good man," she finally whispered. "And a smart one, too." Charlie could never replace Joe— she'd made that clear when he proposed—but surely he deserved as normal a marriage as she could give him. Hadn't she'd just made promises in the rabbi's study to love, honor and cherish? She'd try.

"Let's get Susan tucked in," Rose said.

"No argument there." His voice was lighter now, full of laughter. He swooped the child up and twirled her as he had Rose. Susan squealed as she held Charlie around the neck. "More, Daddy! More!"

She'd made the right decision, thought Rose,

watching them. Charlie hadn't been her first choice for a husband, but in a world turned upside down, he seemed to be her best choice. She had her own family now and a lovely two-bedroom apartment where Susan would have her own room.

It was Charlie who'd insisted on the larger place despite the higher rent. After sleeping on the ground in Europe for so long, he wanted a real bed, not a convertible couch in the living room. Not that they had a couch. In fact, they had no furniture except for the beds, Susan's chifforobe, Rose's grandfather clock and desk, and a bridge table and chairs in the kitchen. Clothes hung in closets; small items lay in boxes on the bedroom floor.

Rose planned to start with window treatments. Simple swags for the living room and bedrooms, a simpler Cape Cod style for the kitchen. Window coverings made a difference between a house and a home.

She helped Susan go through her bathroom routines and toured the new bedroom with her. Then she tucked her into bed, along with all three of her dolls.

"Story?" the child asked hopefully behind her yawns.

"Not tonight, darling," said Rose, lowering herself to sit next to her daughter. "It's too late. Your eyes are closing."

"Two stories tomorrow?" asked Susan.

"Absolutely," said Rose, kissing her good-night. Susan sighed and turned over.

"Mommy! Look."

Rose quickly followed her daughter's gaze but saw nothing unusual until Susan pointed to Joe's picture.

"What, sweetheart?"

The girl bolted upright, her smile wide. "Two daddies! Now I have two daddies."

Rose's heart twisted with such grief, it was as if she were hearing the news about Joe all over again. "Yes, you do," she managed to say. "Daddy Joe—" she swallowed hard "—is sending you his love from heaven. And Daddy Charlie..."

"...is right here, loving you every day with lots of kisses." Charlie leaned over the bed and proceeded to sprinkle his kisses from Susan's head to her toes, including the bottom of her feet, making the child giggle. Her little arms fastened tightly around his neck. Rose's eyes filled with tears.

She'd definitely made the right decision, but...

Suddenly the room darkened. Charlie had turned off the light and was motioning to her.

"She'll be asleep soon," he whispered. "Come on." He left the door ajar, and they returned to the kitchen.

After one look at her, he said, "We have to go forward now, Rose. There's no other way."

She understood the meaning beneath the words. *Bury Joe. Bury him deep so you can live again.*

On this wedding night, she'd try. She owed Charlie that much.

* * *

January 20, 1947

Dear Joe,
Today is Susan's fourth birthday, and I invited the whole family to the new apartment to celebrate. Maybe you're asking, what new apartment? Or maybe you somehow know what's been happening...

I married him, Joe. I married your friend Charlie three months ago. He's a good man, and I can see why you were friends, but he can't replace you. I think people are blessed with only one soul mate, and you and I...well, we were the ones.

Rose paused. She couldn't tell Joe more...about how, on her second wedding night, her body wasn't listening to thoughts about soul mates. In fact, her body seemed to act of its own accord.

She and Charlie had drunk a cup of tea while Susan fell asleep, and then Charlie had asked, "Do you need any help with buttons or laces, Rose?"

She was startled for a second until she realized it was his way of prompting her toward the next part of the evening. She'd known he was a kind person, but now she realized that Charlie Shapiro was smarter than she'd thought. Or very shrewd.

She rose from her chair, pointed to her front-closing jacket. "The buttons are all here. Zipper's on the side. I'm fine."

He grinned and stood up, too. "You're more than fine, Rosie." He leaned forward and kissed her lightly on the mouth. "Take your time. I'm not going anywhere."

She nodded, felt the heat rise to her face and rushed from the kitchen. She grabbed a nightgown and escaped to the bathroom—where she couldn't hide all night. She leaned over the sink, glad her arms supported her. *A normal marriage.* She'd promised herself that her gift to Charlie would be normalcy. She changed into her nightgown quickly, brushed her teeth and unpinned her hair. She studied herself in the mirror—and blinked.

No frowns or worry lines. Her dark eyes shone. A smile seemed to hover. Goodness, she looked young. Eager. She was twenty-five years old and had avoided her reflection in recent times, afraid she'd see the sad, elderly soul she'd become inside. But now...? She wasn't sure how to account for the difference. Marrying Charlie couldn't be the total explanation—that was too simple—and she didn't feel the same way about him as she had about Joe.

With no time for more analysis, she opened the door and called out, "Bathroom's free." Then she walked to the bedroom she'd share with her new husband, sorry now that her flannel nightgown wasn't silk.

"It's October," she whispered to Charlie when he joined her at the window. "I thought I'd be cold."

He burst out laughing. "On our wedding night, Rosie mine, you definitely won't be cold."

Then he'd kissed her while they stood talking, and somehow they were on the bed, covers askew, arms and legs tangled, and like a synchronized explosion…it was done.

Afterward, Charlie perched on his elbow, looking down at her, the cotton top sheet strewn at an angle across her naked body. "Now you know that nightgowns belong on the floor," he whispered. "I love you, Rose. Never forget that."

His words comforted. She nodded and said, "You're a good man, such a good man. We'll move forward now."

He'd lifted her hand to his mouth and kissed her palm. "That's all I ask…for the moment."

I'll be a good wife to him, Joe, of course I will…. He holds you in such high regard that I liked him for that reason alone.

Rose gripped her pen once more and continued her first letter to Joe since her wedding.

Your picture is on Susan's night table. She still says good morning to you each day. Joe, you'd be so proud of her. The child can read! She won't be starting school for another year—she's simply not old enough—but I take her to the library every week, bring home a dozen picture books each time, and we read together.

You'd be proud of Charlie, too. He works hard all day, goes to night school and still volunteers time to resettle displaced persons here in New York. He never talks to me about what happened to him after he was captured, and if someone mentions it, his mouth tightens up and he looks away. I know he hasn't forgotten.

Till the next letter.

Yours forever,

Rose

November 29, 1947

Dear Joe,

Today the United Nations voted with a two-thirds majority to partition Palestine into a Jewish and an Arab state. Sure, most of the land is desert, but we're ecstatic. Now there will be a haven for those who've survived the concentration camps. I think every radio in Brooklyn was tuned to the vote today.

Charlie had tears in his eyes, and he let them fall. He wasn't ashamed; I wasn't, either. Something good has come out of that atrocity. God alone knows what more that madman would have done if our boys had not gone over. I'd rather have you alive, Joe, but you should know that your death was not in vain.

Yours forever,

Rose

* * *

**City University of New York
Baruch College,
School of Business**

**Commencement, January 1949
Ticket of Admission**

Charlie had plans. Big plans. Marching down the aisle in his cap and gown wasn't one of them.

In his opinion, the best part about school had been the other students. Mostly GIs just like him. Brothers through experience who, when they met, communicated with a word, a fragment, a glance or in perfect silence before babbling about their current lives. They tacitly understood the need to focus on the now and on the future.

Maybe some of his school buddies cared about the actual graduation ceremony. Charlie would have preferred the college to send his diploma by mail. Rosie, on the other hand, was definitely excited about the whole event. She'd insisted they all attend his midyear graduation. So now he and Susan were at the front door of the apartment, sweating in their winter coats, waiting for her to appear so they could all go to a boring ceremony.

Tomorrow night would be different. There'd be a family party in his honor—Rose's idea, too. She'd said he deserved a reward for working so hard the past two years, supporting the family and going to school in the evenings. He didn't argue—any reason for a party was okay with him.

The truth was that he didn't need a diploma to earn a good living fixing cars for Texaco. What he did need were golden hands, a sharp eye and ears that could hear the difference between a perfect eight-cylinder purr and a near-perfect purr when the engine turned over. Whether it was luck or talent, he had it all: the hands, the eyes, the ears. And one thing more: he had patience. He got to know each customer's car and its idiosyncrasies just as if he were making a new friend. Ninety-five percent of the time, the new friends turned into old friends, and so did their owners.

Someday, when he bought his own shop, he'd need a business plan and a bank loan. His degree would come in handy when dealing with the suits. Heck, he'd wear one, too, when he walked into the bank.

He glanced at his watch. "Rosie," he called into the back of the apartment, "we need to leave or we'll be late." *Not that I care.*

No answer. "Wait here, honey," he said to Susan, before walking toward the bedroom. But it was the bathroom door that was closed, and he could hear Rose retching on the other side of it. Knocking softly first, he opened the door and there she was on her knees, hugging the toilet and throwing up.

"Oh, sweetheart…" He soaked a washcloth in

cool water and wiped her face, then held her when she heaved again. When she stopped a few minutes later, he helped her up and to their bed.

That's when he saw her tears. Fear kicked in so hard, his stomach felt like a ball of steel. "What is it, Rosie? Tell me what's wrong. Are you sick?"

She shook her head. "I'm not sick. I'm pregnant." Her voice rose in a wail, and she started to cry harder.

A million thoughts, a million feelings tumbled over themselves in him, the biggest one being ecstasy. When he looked at his wife, however, he felt cold, as though a wave of ice water had drenched his soul. She didn't want his baby?

Easy, Charlie. Go carefully. Don't say anything you'll regret. "I thought you wanted a sister or brother for Susan," he said gruffly.

"Of course I do," she mumbled between sobs. "I want to have children with you, but not now! It's not fair. We've been so careful, and Susan's finally in school full-time."

Then it clicked. College. They'd put a plan together. First him. Then her. Part-time at night because days were reserved for only full-time students. Rose had always been the one who craved the formal education, so she could earn a good salary and feel safe. But pregnant women didn't go to school, day or night. And he sure didn't want her running around while she was pregnant.

"I'm sorry, Rose," he said, taking her in his arms. And he was—sort of. He was relieved, however, that her biggest problem was the timing and not about having children. His children.

"Sorry is nice, but you don't understand at all." Her words came fast but, after the nausea, not as strong as his usual Rosie.

"What, sweetheart? What don't I understand?" He continued to hold her, wanting her to know he was listening.

"I can't support us, Charlie, if something should happen to you," she cried. "Susan's government check for war orphans isn't enough even with the money I earn mending clothes. *You're* the bread-winner, Charlie. *You'd* be able to manage without me but I couldn't manage without you, if, God forbid, you get hurt…or worse. How will I earn enough to take care of two children?"

"Nothing's going to happen to me," he said. "The war's over. I'm as healthy as a horse."

She looked at him with such despair, such disappointment, as though *he* were a child. What did she want from him?

"Do you know the future, Charlie?" she asked. "I don't, either. But I know the past."

"Know it, Rosie?" he snapped. "You're still living in it." He was tired of it haunting them, but when he saw the shock on her face, he was ashamed. It was the first time he'd ever lost patience with her.

"I guess the past leaves its mark," he added quietly, "and I can't change that, can I? First the depression years, then losing your husband in the war. Unfortunately there are thousands like you."

"Many of whom are working now, learning new skills," she replied. "But I'm still in the house sewing…and will be… Oh, what's the use of talking?" She gestured her frustration, then rose quickly. "Come on, Charlie. Let's graduate."

"One day, Rosie, I'll be the proudest man in the audience when you march across the stage for your diploma."

"Sure, Charlie. Sure." Stepping through the bedroom door, she called out to Susan, leaving him to follow.

But he couldn't move. Her voice had no life. Her words screamed defeat. She'd given up. Given up on herself, which was so unlike her.

And it was his fault. Well, not exactly, but she was right. Who needed a baby now? He'd rather have his energetic, forward-looking wife back.

The next night saw another first for Rose. Almost everything she served at Charlie's party was store-bought rather than homemade.

"I just lost track of time," she apologized. Actually, she'd needed a three-hour nap that day.

"Food's important," replied Gertie, "but I came to see my family and celebrate my hardworking brother-in-law. That's more important. Besides—" she gestured toward the buffet table in the dining area "—I don't think anyone here will starve."

Rose chuckled as she watched Aaron build a triple-decker roast beef, corned beef and pastrami sandwich with a side of potato salad. Maddy was right behind him with a daintier-size portion.

The doorbell rang again and Rose excused herself. Charlie's parents had arrived.

"Hello, Rose," said Tessie, giving her a perfunctory kiss on the cheek.

"Come in, both of you. Hi, Sam," she added, hugging Charlie's father. She called out to Susan. "Grandma and Grandpa are here."

Susan ran to Sam's open arms like a homing pigeon coming to roost, and Rose marveled, as she often did, that kids always sensed the truth about people. Sam was her grandpa, period.

A chorus of laughter echoed from the living room, and Rose urged the couple inside. "Come join the family. I bet Gertie is telling one of her stories from work."

Tessie sighed. "That sister of yours…aren't you worried? Such a crazy job for a nice girl."

Rosie pasted a smile on her face. "My money's on Gertie. She's as smart as she is quick. In fact, I think she's driving a motorcycle now." Let Tessie absorb that for a while.

"Meshuggener," whispered the older woman, shaking her head. "Crazy."

"Charlie," called Rose. "Why don't you fix your mother a plate of food?"

As she knew he would, Charlie immediately walked toward them, his eyes gleaming with laughter. He knew the routine—when his mom showed up, Charlie became Rose's cavalry, always to the rescue. They'd gone through the scenario many times in the past.

"Come on, Ma," said Charlie now. "Have a sandwich, and I'll show you my diploma."

Tessie's eyes lit up, and Rose swallowed her giggles. Charlie sure could play the woman.

"A college graduate," sighed the proud mother. "Just wonderful."

"You can thank Rosie for that," said Charlie. "She was my inspiration."

"More like your irritation and maybe your aggravation," joked Rose, "pushing you out of the house every school night."

"And why wouldn't you?" Tessie replied sharply. "Education opens doors. Better jobs. More security for…everybody." She pressed her lips together.

"She's all yours," whispered Rose before gliding away. The woman still hadn't forgiven her for marrying her only child, still considered Rose an opportunist. If Rose had turned Charlie down, he would have moved on, met someone else, someone with a clean slate, without a past.

Tessie was foolish not to understand her son after all the years of raising him. Rose had learned in a short time that when Charlie gave his heart, he loved hard. He really did have enough love for the two of them.

Another round of laughter greeted her as she stepped into the living room. Her entire family had come, and as she'd expected, Gertie was in story mode.

"It's been quite a week," Gertie said. "First I'm thrown down the balcony aisle at the Roxy trying to apprehend a raincoat-clad pervert who'd just stolen a woman's purse, among other things."

"Were you hurt? Oh, Gertie..." murmured a chorus of voices.

"Nah. It's my job. Find the pervs and arrest them." She waved away their concerns. "I'm in one piece."

"This time," said Marty, shaking his head. "Just be careful."

"Sure...but listen up. You're not going to believe this," she continued. "Later in the week, I'm at the women's jail with the usual hookers. I'm dressed in full uniform, of course, and one of the girls looks at my badge real hard.

"'Gertrude Kaufman,' the hooker says. And I nod and say, 'That's right.'

"'Well, whaddaya know,' she says."

Gertie looked at each person in Rose's living room. "I swear to God," she continued, "this prostitute who's just been arrested and locked up looks me in the eye and says, in Yiddish no less, 'What's a nice Jewish girl like you doing in a job like that?'"

Rose burst out laughing.

"You're kidding!" said Edith, her eyes bright.

"Could I make this up?"

"So what did you say?" asked Charlie.

"I looked right back at her and asked her the same question. And we both cracked up laughing. Of course, I had to book her, but… hoo-ha, that was a first." Gertie shook her head, closed her eyes and relaxed against the sofa cushions.

Rose studied her sister. Gertie sounded good but looked tired. Her sister's new life seemed to be more taxing than she revealed.

"You have a dangerous job," said Tessie. "It's a crazy choice. Guns. Murderers. Streetwalkers. You could get killed."

"Well, Mrs. Shapiro," Gertie began in a lazy drawl, "I appreciate your feelings, but I think people are crazy to sit behind a desk all day. I couldn't do it."

"And what would your dear mama say about this job? Or your papa, may he rest in peace?"

Silence penetrated to the cracks in the ceiling. Rose's hands fisted, the nails biting into her palms. "Papa knew," she said in defense of her little sister.

Gertie interrupted. "Papa said I should fight for justice and make sure not to arrest the wrong people." She smiled, her eyes shiny. "And then he gave me a blessing and said, '*Gittele,* you're such a smart girl. Maybe you should go back to school and find justice in a courtroom. Become a lawyer. I'll help pay.'"

Rose stood frozen except for her racing heart. She hadn't known about this. Her papa had valued

Gertie more than her. Staying in the house was good enough for Rose. She stepped toward the kitchen.

"I said no, thanks," recalled Gertie. "I didn't have the energy to break more barriers. I told him to help Rose."

Rose halted but didn't turn around.

"What he said was that Rose's job was more important than any of ours. Only she had been entrusted with our future. Only she had been blessed with a child."

"Old-fashioned thinking." Rose hurt, and her voice sounded thick.

"He was an old-world man, Rosie, who valued God and family first, and then education," said Gertie.

"But we live in a new world now," Rose answered. "Doors are opening."

Edith jumped in. "Old world or new," she said, "a child is a blessing more precious than gold. Didn't Mama always say that?" Without waiting for a response, Edith added, "And now Marty and I have an announcement to make."

Discussion forgotten, Rose's heart soared with hope for her older sister. She'd had one miscarriage and no other pregnancies since then. Maybe this time would be lucky.

"I've completed three months," said Edith, her hand stroking her stomach protectively. "I'm very hopeful…and so is the doctor."

As Rose watched, Marty gently turned Edith's face toward him and bestowed such a loving kiss that Rose's eyes filled with tears. The man adored her sister, and Edith returned his love just as fiercely. They were just as she and Joe had been.

She felt Charlie's hands on her shoulders, then he was nuzzling her neck. "Seems like we're not the only ones with news," he whispered.

"Don't say anything yet," she said. "It's Edith's turn in the spotlight. She's so happy."

"I'm happy, too," he replied, "for them. And for us. I know…you're not…"

She got the message. "I may not be thrilled about the timing, but I'll love our baby. I'll be a good mother." It was the most she could offer.

"Good? You're the best. Just look at the little girl we've got. She's perfect because of you."

She understood what he was doing with his compliments—trying to make her feel important. Trying to make her happy when the pregnancy was no more his fault than hers. She sighed heavily and reached for his hand.

"Susan is not quite perfect," Rose said with a smile, "but we'll keep her anyway. She needed a daddy and you're a great one, Charlie. Take some credit."

And then Charlie's lips were on hers, and his kiss rivaled the one Edith had received. Intense, loving…Rose's head swam. She held on to him. It took the whistles and catcalls from around the room to bring her back, and even then, she needed a minute.

"Wow! This is better than any movie at the Roxy.

What's going on here tonight?" asked Gertie. "Any more announcements we should know about?"

Suddenly the room stilled, an air of expectation hanging over it.

"Rosie?" Charlie breathed her name.

She nodded. Gertie had provided an opening too perfect to ignore.

"As a matter of fact," began Charlie, "Susan is going to have a little brother or sister."

Charlie's joy radiated from his whole being as he picked Susan up and held her in his arms, his grin huge. "Did you hear that, Susie Q? You're going to be a big sister."

"Or a brother," she said.

Not quite, but Rosie didn't correct her.

"Mazel tov! Mazel tov!" Congratulations from their family filled the air. Except for Tessie, who seemed dumbstruck. Finally.

Chapter 6

January 20, 1949

Dear Joe,

It's late at night, and our guests for Susan's party have gone home. Our daughter is six years old! She's one of the oldest in her kindergarten class and reads so well I think she belongs in first grade instead.

I have so much to tell you. As usual, your parents joined us for the birthday party. Susan loves them, Joe, and they adore her. She understands now that Daddy Joe is their boy.

From the minute they arrived, Susan received their undivided attention, but I'm not worried about them spoiling her. Can there be such a thing as too much love? I don't think so. I think the more loving adults a child has, the greater the security and confidence in the child. In many ways, Susan is lucky.

Your sister and her new husband came, too. I don't see Sarah as much as I used to...it's a bit awkward. When she looks at Charlie, I know she's thinking of you. We share so many years of memories...

I have something to tell you...and I hope you understand.

I'm pregnant, Joe, due next July. I almost feel guilty, but my brain says that's ridiculous—and my heart needs to listen. Charlie and I have as good a marriage as most. I guess we suit one another in a day-to-day sort of way. I know he was someone you relied on in your unit—at least to sing the men to sleep! That's what he told me.

How do I tell your parents about the new baby? Susan and I visit them whenever we can but not as often since we moved from the old neighborhood. Charlie fixes cars, but we don't own one yet. Maybe I should tell Sarah first, and we can figure it out together.

More news... As of last week, I'm once again married to a college man. That's right. Charlie graduated from the CUNY business school, but you have left your mark on him, too. He often reads Shakespeare's plays—especially the tales you told.

And me? Well, I'll have to wait a little longer to catch up to both of you as a college grad.

Yours forever,

Rose

From the bedroom doorway, Charlie watched Rose remove the cover of that—that Dream Box, she called it. Very pretty, but it had nothing to do with him. It was all about Joe. She cherished the thing, handled it as though it were fragile porcelain. And now she was reading Joe's letters again, lost in the past. Silently, he slipped away and returned to the kitchen, immaculate again after Susan's birthday party.

He had no right to be disappointed that Rose still missed Joe, but he was. Charlie and she had been married over two years now, and he'd gotten to know her habits. That Dream Box was one of them. She took it out from time to time, and not only on Susan's birthday. He could understand revisiting Joe on his daughter's birthday, but how many times during the year did she have to read his letters? By now she must have memorized them.

Hells bells! He needed some air.

"Charlie-e."

Rose stood on the kitchen threshold, her wavy dark hair brushing the collar of her pink nightgown, a soft smile on her face.

"Are you coming to bed now, Charlie?" A yawn took her by surprise. "My, oh my, I am so tired."

With one glance at her, his frustration disappeared. She was beautiful, sweet and pregnant with his child. As his mother would say, he'd made his bed, now he had to lie in it. Fortunately, when he held Rose in his arms, he had no desire to lie anywhere else. Maybe one day he wouldn't be disappointed anymore. Maybe one day he wouldn't be competing with Joe.

He held out his hand. "Come on, Rosie mine. I'll tuck you in."

"That sounds lovely. I probably shouldn't say it, but Susan's birthday is always so…so…exhausting."

He studied her expression. Beyond her fatigue was something more—shadows, sadness. From revisiting Joe? But he wouldn't assume anything. It wasn't his business. Besides, if Rose wanted to talk, she would.

"We had a houseful today," he offered. "It was too much for you."

She cocked her head, stared at him. "Sure. That's probably all it is." She let go of his hand. "Well, good night, Charlie." And she left him alone in the kitchen.

She'd shut him out faster than it took him to snap his fingers. Damn it! He wasn't a mind reader, and he wouldn't nag. Obviously something was bothering her, but if she didn't trust him enough to share her thoughts, so be it.

She was pulling down the bedspread when he entered the bedroom. "I'm going for a walk, Rose."

She snapped around. "A walk? It's thirty degrees outside."

"I won't be long. Just need to stretch my legs."

She looked hard at him again, then shrugged. "So go stretch. I'm going to sleep."

He turned and left the room, his jaw tight. Why didn't she ask him to stay?

Rose gazed at his retreating back, tears welling in her eyes. Sure she was tired. Being pulled between the past and present would make a person tired. Not to mention the pregnancy.

She shut off the bedside lamp and lay in the dark, allowing her tears to roll down her face. She'd almost told him about the letters she wrote to Joe. Knowing Charlie, he would have been a good listener, wanting to help her figure out things. But just as she was on the verge of confiding, he'd made other excuses for her. His wishes were clear—he'd seen the Dream Box, and he didn't want to discuss Joe.

She adjusted her pillow and pulled the covers up high, trying to settle in. A married woman shouldn't feel so lonely. A married woman shouldn't be in bed by herself. If only…if only Joe… Her throat ached as she worked to control her sobs. A losing battle.

Her tears were down to a trickle when she heard Charlie unlock the front door. He was back. Turning on her stomach, she wrapped her arms around her pillow and inhaled smoothly, then exhaled, imitating the rhythm of sleep.

She heard his light step in the hall, heard the bathroom door close. *Now get to sleep.* She yawned and finally allowed herself to drift off. Charlie then came into the bedroom and started to hum quietly. She didn't know whether to laugh or cry. "La Vie En Rose." Edith Piaf's song. He'd translated it for her once, so now Charlie had declared it was also *her* song. She never knew when the French refrain would stir the air the way it did now, so very softly as he prepared for bed.

"*Quand elle me prend dans ses bras…*"

The mattress dipped as he sat down.

"La, la la la la la la…" he sang.

The blanket lifted, and he lay beside her.

"I see *la vie en rose*," he finished on a whisper.

The words came from above so he must be staring down at her. His gentle kiss on her cheek confirmed it. "Are you really sleeping, Rosie?"

"Yes," she said.

When he chuckled, her whole body sank deeper into the mattress. "No more walks, Charlie," she murmured.

A moment of silence filled the room, then Charlie said, "Love words, Rosie? That's a gift I'll engrave forever in my heart."

Love words? Couldn't be… But she had no time for reflection as Charlie's kisses feathered her cheek while his hand stroked her back and found its way beneath her nightgown. His fingers brushed across her already tender breasts. Three strokes were all it took and she was on fire. Which was crazy, but…

"Take off my panties," she said, wriggling to help.

"My pleasure."

When he stripped off his own clothes, she was more than ready for him. And when he entered her, they locked together like pieces in a puzzle with no need for spoken language.

They moved as one, neither one leading, neither one following, and she climaxed almost immediately—before Charlie did. This lovemaking was unusual but exciting. Just as exciting to watch his face, the tension, the taut lips as he reached his point of release.

And all because of her. The thought jammed her mind, totally unexpected. Totally powerful.

"My God, you're something." Charlie's admiration confirmed her idea, but somehow, however, it didn't sit well.

"It's the pregnancy," she replied quickly. "I don't know what's gotten into me." It was stupid to feel embarrassed with her own husband.

"It's more than the pregnancy, Rosie," he said, stroking her face, his index finger brushing her lips. "Making love is healthy for us, beyond the happiness of conceiving children. It reminds us that we're alive. It's a miracle to me every single time."

He never failed to surprise her, this man who fixed cars for a living, who came home with grease imbedded in his skin, and who sprouted ideas that could seed conversations for hours. Maybe his seemingly endless depth had to do with his war experience.

"That's pretty philosophical, Charlie," she said slowly. "I was just thinking about this—" she motioned at the bed "—but I've never thought about intimacy quite the way you do." She leaned back against her pillow. "I've just sort of…you know, uh, enjoyed it."

"Then I'm a lucky man," he said.

"If you think so," said Rose, "I won't argue." And she wouldn't. Charlie might pretend to forget the past, but she never forgot that he'd entered marriage with a handicap. She almost said he wore rose-colored glasses, but stopped herself in time. He'd latch on to the bad pun and drive her nuts.

"You're an interesting man, Charlie. You think about a lot of different things."

"Two compliments in one night?" he joked. "I promise they won't go to my head, Rosie, especially since most guys think about only one thing all day long—the same thing—and that is women. They're just too polite to say so, but if a pretty woman walks by…well, let's say that every mother's son will stand at attention."

She started to giggle at the image. "Before they get married, you mean?"

Charlie's hearty laugh came from deep inside, full of warmth, amusement and light until he had to wipe away a tear. "Oh, Rosie, Rosie," he said. "You grew up surrounded by sisters and a brother too young to enlighten you. Well, I won't either. Give me a kiss and go to sleep, my beautiful wife."

She wouldn't argue with him about this. She had lived a family-oriented and, she supposed, rather sheltered life. Everybody did in those Williamsburg brownstones where each day's routines—prayer, meals, school, chores, work—incorporated the struggle to survive. She didn't know everything about men-and-women relationships, so she'd keep her mouth shut except for one item.

"I don't need compliments, Charlie. You've got eyes. I'm not beautiful. Edith is the lovely one. Gertie's the cute one. I'm just in the middle."

"Just? What are you talking about? There's no 'just.' The middle's the best part of the sandwich!"

She turned over and grinned. The man could make her laugh.

"Rosie?"

"Hmm?"

"Did you put your crackers on the night table for tomorrow morning?"

"Yes. The nausea's getting easier." He was thoughtful for asking.

"Good."

Actually, life was good enough at the moment. She finally slept, her dreams not of husbands but of babies.

"Edith, I've been to the nursery. She's perfect and beautiful, too!"

Edith looked up at Rose from her hospital bed. "A month early, she's a little small. Just five pounds."

"But she's healthy, so she's simply…petite.

She'll grow now." Rose lowered herself heavily into the guest chair.

"I think so, too. I can't wait for her next feeding."

Of course she couldn't. Edith was thirty-three years old and this was her first child.

"How are you feeling, Rose? Your maternity clothes are so stylish—you have a gift with that needle—but you look so uncomfortable."

"Two months more," she sighed. "The weather's so hot for May, even the lightest material sticks to me. Charlie bought a big box fan, and I sit in front of it most of the day sewing, except when I walk Susan to school." She glanced at her watch. "I have exactly twenty minutes to visit before I have to go meet her."

Edith's gaze wandered past Rose, and a beatific smile lit her face. "Marty! I didn't expect you during the day. What a nice surprise."

"And how's my beautiful bride?" he said, swooping down to kiss Edith. He turned and kissed Rose, too. "And my beautiful sister-in-law?"

"The whole world's beautiful to you, Daddy," teased Rose. "My niece is gorgeous."

"Looks just like her mother," Marty replied, gazing at his wife. "Have you told Rosie the name yet?"

Edith shook her head and looked at Rose. "We're naming her Anna, after Mama. Just Anna, all by itself. No middle name. So it's special."

Rose blinked hard. "A perfect choice. I wish… how I wish…" She shook her head. "Oh, my. Mama is missing so much…Susan growing up and the new babies… And how I miss her—her wisdom and common sense—myself." Her tears began to trickle. *She would have helped me through all the changes in my life.*

"I know, Rosie. I know. Don't cry, or I'll start to cry with you. We're too emotional now." Edith took a deep breath. "So, if you have a boy this time… then a name for Papa?"

"Definitely. Papa needs a namesake, and Charlie's parents are still alive and well."

"I was talking to Charlie last night," said Marty. "Did he tell you?"

"What?" said Rose. "I heard him on the phone while I was giving Susan a bath, but couldn't make out the words. Was it important?"

Her brother-in-law sat on the side of the bed, his expression eager.

"More good news, Rose. We're going to move by next spring. To Queens. Brand-new co-op apartments are going up. Instead of paying rent, we'll buy one and own it. If something breaks, the maintenance department fixes it. It's an investment…"

"The apartments are awfully nice," Edith chimed in. "I saw the blueprints. There's even one layout with three bedrooms, and the rooms are big. An elementary school is close by—two blocks away. We were hoping you and Charlie might want to buy one, too."

But Rose was still back at Marty's first sentence. "You're moving? Out of Brooklyn?"

"Not to Mars, Rosie, just to Queens," said Marty. "Think about it. A new beginning in this new world of ours. Anything is possible now that the war is over."

"Queens…?" The news was so unexpected, she had a hard time taking the "good" part in.

"It's attached to Brooklyn, Rose…" Marty continued to tease. "You know, one of the five boroughs that comprise New York City."

It wasn't the geography that bothered her. "Changes," she whispered. "More changes. I don't know."

"Just think about it," said Edith as Rose stood, preparing to leave.

"What about Aaron and Maddy?" asked Rose. "Have you spoken with them? Are they moving, too?"

"Yes. And no," Marty answered. "They have bigger plans."

"Bigger plans?" Another jolt. "What? Where? Why am I the last to know everything?"

Edith answered her. "Because I make the most phone calls. If I waited for Gertie or Aaron to call, I'd never know what's going on in our family."

Once again Rose was reminded that Edith was the oldest, shouldering the self-imposed responsibility of keeping tabs on everyone, keeping the family together.

Rose leaned over her sister and kissed her on the cheek. "I love you, Edith. Be well. And I'll think about…Queens."

* * *

> **ROSE and CHARLIE SHAPIRO**
> present
> **"IT'S A BOY!"**
> Starring
> **STEVEN JOEL**
> Saturday, July 15, 1949, at 12:15 p.m.
> Weight: 7 lb. 2 oz. Hair: Auburn Eyes: Blue
>
> The management reserves the right
> to cancel personal appearances if
> the star is sleeping or eating.

Rose kept the Dream Box on the shelf of her bedroom closet. The original packaging still protected the wood-and-silver filigree work on the cover. She protected it further from the dust by placing it inside a white plastic bag.

She reached for that plastic bag now, a month after her son's birth, and in a moment, she was seated at her familiar desk, the Dream Box in front of her.

August 12, 1949

Dear Joe,
Susan has a little brother named after Papa and you. That's right. You. I'm glad about it, but to be truthful, it was not my idea. It was Charlie's. He said that Susan would have more patience with a little brother if she knew her daddy Joe was connected to the baby.

Rose paused, the tip of her pen in her mouth. Her husband was the most cheerful of men, knew everyone in the neighborhood, but when his serious side emerged, no one could change his course. He was still donating time to resettling refugees from Europe despite marriage, work, school and fatherhood. And now this, their baby's name.

"You want to name your son after Joe?" she'd asked, not quite believing she'd understood him.

"His sister has no children yet—maybe she never will. Should I leave Joe without a name? It's bad enough he's buried thousands of miles away where no one can visit his grave."

When she was about to protest, he interrupted. "Yes, yes. I understand," he said. "It's not really for Joe at all. It's for *me*. It makes me feel better not to think of him so alone." He paused for a moment, then added with a catch in his voice, "Joe was my friend, too, Rose. I don't forget my friends."

So your parents came to the bris, *and we named the baby Shimon Yosef and chose Steven Joel in English. We're all happy. Before the circumcision, your mother told me to dip the corner of a handkerchief in some wine and let the baby suck on it so he'd be too busy to cry. It worked!*

You must have had a strong friendship with Charlie. I bet you understood him better than I do. The longer I live with him, the more I learn, but the more there is to discover. On the surface, you get only what you see, like a beautiful oil painting viewed from a distance. It's only when you get closer that you notice how it's built with layer upon layer of brush-strokes. I think Charlie has a lot of layers that I haven't noticed.

You and I, well, we knew each other for years because you were Sarah's brother. Marriage to you was easy and natural. Comfortable. Marriage to Charlie is laced with the unknown, and I don't like surprises.

Rose looked over what she'd written and nodded. As always when she wrote to Joe, she spilled her worries, her thoughts, every word coming straight from her heart. Tonight, despite a new baby in the house, almost everything she told Joe centered around Charlie. Interesting that she'd reveal so much of her second husband to her first. She felt a pang of guilt. Maybe she shouldn't be so open. Maybe Joe wouldn't want to know.

She sighed, placed one of her son's baby announcements in the Dream Box, signed and folded the letter, placing it inside, too. She could barely close the lid; she'd need to create a new place for her notes. Just as she slid the package into its plastic bag, she heard Charlie's footsteps.

"Rose, I thought you'd be asleep— Oh. Your treasure chest." His tone was flat.

"I put the birth announcement inside," she replied. "For safekeeping."

Slowly she saw the warmth return to his eyes and a smile cross his face. "Well, that's smart, Rosie. Very smart."

He approached her, leaned over and gave her a kiss on the cheek.

"That was a good day, Charlie, at the *bris*," she said, standing up and replacing the Dream Box in the closet. "The whole family was together—yours, mine, even Joe's."

"Every day is a good day, Rosie. But yes, it was special. How are you feeling today?"

"Strong as a horse. Don't worry about me."

"A horse? You look great, but don't overdo it. So, are you ready for more good news?"

She braced herself. Charlie's definition of *good news* was not necessarily hers. "Should I sit down first?"

"Oh, you're going to like this. As of tomorrow, we will be the proud owners of a brand-spanking-new 1949 Studebaker. Our own car, Rosie. What do you say to that?"

He looked as eager as a boy, but her stomach tightened and the words stuck in her throat. She could barely whisper, "How much, Charlie? How much did it cost?"

"We have the money, Rose. Eight hundred fifty dollars. Not so bad for a man who earns a living with cars. Besides, it's less than the apartment costs."

He was going too fast for her. She lowered herself to the edge of the bed. "The co-op in Queens? We haven't discussed that in a long time." She hadn't even thought about it since before Steven was born.

"We can do both, Rosie. Marty told me last Sunday that he and Edith put a down payment on a two-bedroom. It faces west. From the fifth floor they'll see the Empire State Building, the whole skyline of Manhattan."

"But with a new car, Charlie, we can stay here and visit Edith and Marty whenever we want." She heard the panic in her own voice; Charlie must have heard it, too. He sat down next to her and patted her hand.

"Why don't you just think about it, Rose? Take some time. The two baby cousins could grow up together. Edith would love for you to be close."

"But you work in Brooklyn…"

"So, I can drive to the shop instead of taking a bus. We'll figure it out. Just think about it."

2007

"Think about it?" repeated Rose to her audience in the kitchen. "You know when Charlie gets an idea in his head, that's it. Done! And *poof!*" She clapped her hands for emphasis. "We were in Queens."

"Dad, I'm surprised she didn't poison you!" said Susan, laughing. "Forcing her to go."

"Well, that's not exactly how it happened," said

Charlie, leaning back in his chair. "Sure, I prodded a little, but that didn't do any good right away."

"Hmm," said Rose, "he may be correct. I was frightened of anything to do with spending money. Always in the back of my mind, I thought…what if? What if I were alone again? I had two children to support at that time and still no education to have a career. How would I make ends meet?"

She paused for a moment, looked out the window to the spacious backyard, trees dressed in shades of red, orange, yellow and brown. Autumn in New York. She glanced around the kitchen at the resilient countertops she'd had installed, at the country-style, French-tile backsplash. She pictured some favorite items scattered throughout the house. Brooklyn seemed a lifetime away. It was.

"You might think I was foolish," she said to her daughter, "knowing what you know now. How it all worked out in the end. Here Dad and I sit in a lovely home, our children blessed with health, intelligence and wonderful families of their own. But…at the time, I was frightened. I'd had too many losses, too many changes in my life, and despite Daddy's good job, I still thought my world could come to an end if we didn't save every possible dollar he earned."

"Just in case…" said Paul.

Rose nodded. "Exactly right. With me, everything was 'just in case.'"

"So, tell them what changed your mind, Rosie." Charlie glanced at her before pouring himself another cup of coffee. "And tell the truth. This time, it wasn't me."

Automatically, Rose patted her stomach. "Anita. I was pregnant again. And miserably sick. I wanted to stay in bed all day. But God bless Edith, she kept saying the apartments were selling like hot cakes. Buy one."

"Finally, we grabbed a three-bedroom," said Charlie, "almost the last one available. So Aunt Edith and Anita were the real motivators."

"We moved in 1951, a year after Edith and Marty, and Anita was born in early '52. In the middle of a snowstorm."

"Naturally," said Susan with a sigh. "Why is there so much drama in this family?"

"Drama?" said Charlie. "That's nonsense, and you know better. It's called living a life. That's what it's about for every family."

"Well, it's giving me a chronic headache," said Susan, rubbing her temple. "Liz pregnant and Matt going off to a war zone. We don't need that drama. Maybe this headache will disappear when he comes home again." She paused, then put her head in her hands and groaned. "*If* he comes home again. My daughter, my wonderful daughter. She loves him so much. If anything happens to him…"

Silence fell for a moment. Then Rose said, "She'll survive. I guarantee it."

"The proof's in there," said Charlie, pointing to the Dream Box. "She's a proud ship loaded with cargo."

Susan reached toward the box, her slender fingers rubbing the wood, then gently traveling across the silver garlands. "It's so pretty, and yet, I hated this thing," she said. "Did you know, Mom, I always cried when you took it off the shelf?"

As her daughter's words sank in, Rose couldn't move—not a finger, not a toe. Her throat, too, felt frozen, but she managed to say in a voice peppered with gravel, "You cried, Susie? But why?"

Susan picked up the golden thimble Charlie had given Rose when he courted her. Next she reached for Charlie's graduation ticket, then her brother's birth announcement.

"Maybe I've always been too emotional...I remember too much—like the night *Zayde* died. The room had been dark, and a small lamp burned in the corner, casting long shadows. I'd climbed on top of him and yelled at him to wake up, but he didn't. And nobody came for a long time." She glanced at Rose, then Charlie. "Until finally, you both were there."

Through the open window, Rose heard the song of a common sparrow. It irritated her and she wanted to cover her ears. What could she have done back then for Susan? What had she missed?

But Susan was on to the next topic, and Rose kept quiet.

"I remember Aunt Edith and Uncle Marty's wedding. I remember Dad's graduation from college and how we were so late they almost didn't let him walk down the aisle. I remember when Anna was born and the big fuss over her. And I thought, 'Maybe Aunt Edith won't love me anymore.'"

"Edith adored you as much as I did," Charlie said. "You were everybody's child. Everybody's hope."

"Children always are," admitted Susan, "but I didn't understand that at the time. I thought I was competing with Anna."

"Oh, honey, my sister was too smart for that."

Susan chuckled. "She sure was. She 'counted' on me to help her take care of my cousin, to read to her. And then, of course, came Steven and our house was so busy.

"I remember all of it, but most of all, Mom, I remember the letters in the Dream Box. That's what made me cry." Susan glanced at the box again quickly before standing up and fumbling through the fridge.

"How could that be, Susie? You never read those letters," said Rose.

"That didn't matter," her daughter replied, bringing a package of cheese to the table. She took the carafe of coffee and began refilling her cup, but her hand trembled and she returned the pot to its holder. She stared at Rose.

"I saw your face when you studied those letters, those papers which were so important to you. You didn't hide your feelings. You were sad, so...so... melancholy. I cried because I didn't know how to make you happy. And I was afraid to ask you."

Tears welled in Rose's eyes, and with the first

blink, they trickled down her cheek. She snatched a napkin and blotted. This was a surprise she could have done without on the day before her sixtieth wedding anniversary. Before she could find words, however, Charlie interrupted her effort.

"If it makes you feel any better, Susie Q, you weren't alone. I didn't know what to do either, except forge ahead. Your mother," he continued, "has always been the one for me. The *only* one for me. So I had no choice but to go on and hope for the best."

"And here we are," Susan said. "But at the time, I didn't understand that a child is not responsible for a parent's happiness."

"But is a parent responsible for a child's happiness?" asked Paul, his words quick, his voice sharp. Rose knew he was thinking of Liz and Matt and their ongoing conflict with Susan, who was still insisting on repaying Matt's loans.

"We do the best we can, Paul," Rose said. "No one starts out to be a lousy parent."

Susan's laugh was dry. "Mom's right, but... maybe I work too much. Maybe I'm too bossy.... Maybe I didn't give enough time to the kids, and now they won't listen."

Charlie's laughter boomed. "How do you win a Pulitzer Prize without working hard? How do you write book after book without working hard? And teach at the university, and host *History, Live!* on public radio? The passion is good, Susie Q. It's who you are."

"But perhaps there's been a cost… Oh my God, Paul! Have I not paid enough attention to you, too?"

In a second, Paul had his arms around her. "Who's the drama queen now, Suze? Don't be an idiot. I love you to pieces and you're a great mother. What are you doing to yourself?"

Susan peeked up at her husband. "You know what they say about an unexamined life…"

Rose's lips twitched, but she sat very still. She'd spent her life weighing and measuring, judging and trying to do the right things, but she tasted the bitter flavor of Susan's last question. There had been a time she took Charlie for granted. A time when she hadn't paid enough attention.

She reached into the Dream Box, pulled out a worn piece of paper and unfolded it. She laid it on the table so her family could see….

PART TWO

Queens

Chapter 7

"**K**eep this safe, Rose," said Charlie, placing the bill of sale for the new apartment on their kitchen table. "It's an anniversary present to ourselves. Look here. See the date—October 15, 1951. Five years together and we're moving up."

"It's not like we live in a Quonset hut right now," she replied, motioning to the rest of the apartment. "You make the new place sound like the Garden of Eden. It's a new neighborhood, with new people, and we'll have another baby. Child number three."

"Exactly the point, Rosie. We're living in a new world, a world of opportunity, and there's a baby boom going on. Our kids will have lots of friends. The schools are close. You'll see. You'll be happy."

She glared at him. "Susan has friends here."

"The monthly payments are low, Rosie, and they can't go up without permission of the board of directors. We own shares in the co-op."

He'd hit her tender spot. "And that's the only reason, besides the third bedroom, that I'm agreeing to this. I like having a say in the finances. I'm not a woman you can just schlep along with all your ideas."

"Oh, Rosie, I definitely know that. I would never dream of simply schlepping you along." But his hazel eyes danced with light, and the corners of his mouth twitched with suppressed laughter.

Rosie started giggling. Then Charlie's hearty tones joined hers. And suddenly she was in his arms, waltzing, listening to him woo her again. "'I'm gonna love you, da, da, da da, da-dum, Come rain or come shine...'"

He believed it, he wanted her to believe it. And if he had been her first husband, it would have been very easy.

"You could have been a cantor in the shul with that beautiful voice," she said.

"The next Al Jolson, huh? From the synagogue to showbiz. Uh-uh, not for me. I'd rather putter around with engines and sing only to you."

"Don't forget the children. As soon as Stevie hears your lullaby, he settles in and falls asleep. Really, Charlie. It's like magic." She leaned against him as they continued dancing.

"He's some kid, isn't he?" His voice reverberated against her ear; she felt his chest swell. If buttons could really pop, Charlie's shirt would have sprung open.

Rose chuckled. "Do you think I'll say otherwise?"

she replied. "Steven's the best. But no more children after this next one." She stopped dancing and patted her stomach. Her tone hardened as the frustration she normally kept to herself flowed to the surface.

"I'm telling you now, Charlie, after I deliver this one, I'm done."

"You talk like it's my fault," he protested. "It was an accident. We used protection, and it failed."

"Then we'll use two or three kinds. I'm thirty years old, Charlie. When is it my turn?"

He didn't answer for a moment, then said, "You're like a broken record. I'm sorry you're unhappy, Rose, but what do you want me to do? I can't change history, and I'm working as hard as I can to give us a good life. We both love kids, and if you want to know the truth, I think your pregnancy is a good kind of accident."

She whirled away from him. "A good kind?" How could he not understand? "If it's so good, then you can take care of this one when it's born. Mark my words, Charlie—I am going to night school next fall, and you can handle all three of them."

"My pleasure," he replied without hesitation. "I'm surprised, however, that you're still playing catch-up with your sisters. You're the smartest one of all."

"Save your compliments." With hands on her hips, she stared him down. "Even though they both have careers, my sisters aren't the issue. Think, Charlie. Do you suppose I'm happy mending other people's clothes for a few dollars here and there?

The factories are doing the big jobs. And husbands don't just die in wars. Didn't Marvin Cohen die after a heart attack last year? He was only forty-eight years old. Supporting two children would be hard enough, but how would I manage with three? The small life insurance wouldn't last a minute. So don't look at me as if I'm the selfish one here, Charles Shapiro. Try looking in the mirror."

Her heart pounded so hard that, in the stillness that followed, she barely heard Susan crying.

When she turned she saw her daughter crouching on the floor right outside the kitchen. As Rose stepped toward her, Susan jumped to her feet.

"Stop it! Stop it. No more yelling. I don't like it." Her sobs were punctuated with hiccups, her chin trembled. But it was her eyes—those big dark eyes so like Joe's—now shadowed and filled with fear, that crushed Rose's heart. Stole her breath. Charlie scooped the child up before Rose could get her. With one arm around Charlie's neck, Susan reached toward Rose with the other.

In tandem, they kissed and comforted.

"That was only loud talking," said Rose. "Sometimes it happens."

"No," said Susan. "No."

Charlie glanced at Rose and murmured, "Back me up." He kissed Susan again. "We agree. There will be no more yelling in this family. It's over."

"Mommy?" Susan said, her voice unsure.

Rose melted. "Of course, no more yelling. We'll

only discuss from now on." In the future, she and Charlie would "discuss" behind closed doors, where her daughter couldn't hear.

"Good," said Susan. "I want everybody to be happy like in Aunt Edith's house."

"Well, this is your house," said Charlie, blowing a raspberry on her belly. When she giggled, Rose sighed with relief. "And this is where you belong."

"Good," she said again.

"Now, into bed with you, Susie Q."

"Could I have a glass of water first?"

Her daughter was back to normal.

Thirty minutes later, as she and Charlie climbed into their own bed, Rose said, "Spats are normal between a husband and wife."

"Our Susie is too young to understand that."

Rose sighed. "Too young and too sensitive. I wish I could toughen her up…"

"Let her be, Rose. She is who she is. Just like we all are." He patted her stomach. "Each one is unique. A surprise package."

"Well, I hope this one takes after its brother. Steven's been a perfect baby. Eating, sleeping, playing. Goes down for a nap. I'd like a carbon copy, please."

January 20, 1952

Dear Joe,

I'm running a small party for Susan on her ninth birthday. Family only. I'll soon deliver the new baby, so I'm not in great shape to host a gala event.

We're in our new place now. Charlie hired a moving company to do all the hard work. Everyone else in my family came to help with the rest. When we got to the new apartment, they unpacked, too. I didn't have to do a thing except watch the kids and give orders, which Charlie says I'm very good at.

Susan helped me with her brother. She's very patient, maybe because she's looking forward to having a bedroom of her own again.

I'm going back to school in the fall. Charlie and I have a deal—he'll babysit if I get A's. Some deal. He thinks I can do anything—which is very good for my ego. We'll see what happens.

Oh, I almost forgot. There's talk about your commander in chief, Dwight D. Eisenhower, running for president of the United States in this year's election. A chicken in every pot, a car in every garage—that's the theme for the future. Unfortunately war is never out of date. No sooner did the boys come home than we had troubles in Korea and our soldiers were sent there to fight. So now we have a "cold war" going on: Russia and communism vs.

the U.S.A., capitalism and democracy. Funny
how an ally can turn into an enemy so quickly.
I'll keep you posted.

Yours forever,
Rose

P.S.   Did I ever tell you about Gertie and
Dan? Daniel O'Brien. That's right. As
Irish a name as you can imagine. But
you know how it goes with Gertie—
nothing's ever simple and straightfor-
ward.

Dan is a cop in the same precinct as my
sister. Of course, there are lots of men
working there, but Dan had his eye on
her, and she'd noticed him, too. However,
she was cautious. She'd been burned
once before with an Irish-Catholic boy-
friend whom she was crazy about, but
whose mother wasn't crazy about her.
The relationship ended, and Gertie,
who's used to being liked by everybody,
wasn't herself for a while.

So she didn't exactly encourage Dan
O'Brien. But he had a surprise for her.
On Passover last year, she went to work
and there in the break room, Dan was
chomping away on a piece of matzoh
covered with peanut butter. He offered
Gertie the box and the jar. She thought

he was trying to impress her, but it
turned out his mother's Jewish. His dad's
a cop, too.
Leave it to Gertie. The wedding's in June.

Rosie's new daughter was definitely not a carbon copy of Steven. Colicky and constantly crying, the infant would have been a challenge to anyone. To Rose's surprise, however, and despite her rants about this unexpected baby, a surge of maternal instinct sprang from inside her—the poor child was in such pain.

"Come here, my beautiful girl," she cooed, turning Anita facedown on her lap and rubbing her back. Instantly, the baby's cries lessened. "That's what you needed, my *shayna maidele*. A little pressure on the belly."

And so it went, changing positions, changing formulas, even trying goat's milk instead of cow's milk. Nothing really worked. After two months of the baby's crying, Rose and Charlie were both exhausted. Every night, they alternated rocking Anita in the carriage, which seemed to work, until they stopped the motion. As soon as they tiptoed away, the baby cried again.

"You know what, Mommy," whispered Susan one Saturday evening while sitting on Rose's bed, watching her rock the carriage.

"What, sweetheart?"

"Sometimes, I feel sorry for you and Daddy."

"Better to feel sorry for your sister. Her belly hurts."

"I know," Susan sighed. "And we can't make it better. The doctor said we just have to wait. That's why I'm sad for you. You and Daddy always make things better. You *like* to make things better."

Once again, a comment from Susan made Rose pause. She had to jot it down for Joe. This daughter of theirs—where did she get her ideas? Did other children think as she did?

"Taking care of you and the babies is our job, Susie Q," said Rose. "I love you and Steven and Anita no matter what."

"No matter how much she cries?"

"Absolutely. We're not giving her back!" she teased.

"Good." Susan stretched out on the bed, yawned and rolled over on her stomach. She blinked at her mother once, twice, and her eyes closed.

Susan would sleep well that night, thought Rose. She'd unwrapped her worries for her mother's inspection. Give back Anita? Charlie really had to stop joking about that. As Rose had always suspected, Susan was a worrier. Just like her mother had become since Joe had marched off to war.

On a beautiful Sunday in June 1952, when Anita was four months old, Rose gathered the two younger children for an afternoon in the park behind the local elementary school. Susan was visiting with her two best girlfriends in the building and would be occupied for a few hours.

Charlie had already left to pick up the *New York Times* and would meet her at the park. Edith and Marty would bring Anna, and the kids could run around, play on the swings and seesaw. Perhaps some of their neighbors would have the same idea. Rose had made some new friends in her building, and so had Edith in her building around the corner. Almost all the residents were young families with children. Lots of children. Susan's class had thirty-eight students.

Rose dressed in a pink cotton shirtwaist, stockings and a pair of wedged espadrilles. A light breeze flowed over her as she wheeled the baby down the avenue. Anita had fallen asleep, and Steven was singing to himself as he walked beside her, hanging on to the carriage handle. At that moment, under the summer sun, Rose was at peace.

Until she turned the corner.

A crowd had gathered at the curb about twenty feet from where she stood. Automatically, her stomach tightened, and she walked faster, Stevie trotting to keep up. Had there been an accident? Where was Charlie?

Weird. The group consisted only of men. They were in a circle looking down at something. As she got closer, she saw the hood of a car was up, and she was able to identify the "something." Her husband. Charlie was leaning under the hood of someone's car and lecturing the men. She didn't understand a word of what he was saying, but most of the guys seemed to or were trying to. Some were nodding, the others were listening and listening hard. As she walked by, two more people joined the crowd.

Charlie could hold an audience, and it seemed that owning a car, driving a car and caring for a car thrilled the hearts of every man in the neighborhood. Maybe on the planet. Automobiles were a big deal, and her husband was in the thick of it.

Not a bad thing. She waved as she passed by. "Take your time," she said. Whether he was testing the waters or simply being friendly, she didn't know and she wouldn't interfere. Not yet. But if Charlie ever reached the point of leaving Texaco to start his own business as he'd been hinting, she fully intended to help him make the final decision.

Charlie bided his time before springing his deed on Rose. A colicky baby followed by the hot summer last year could fray anyone's nerves. The fall had brought relief, at least with the weather, and it had brought some excitement to his wife as she prepared to return to City College. But Susan had come home from school with the chicken pox in early September.

"Better chicken pox than polio," Rose had said, her mouth tight.

"Amen."

They'd shipped Anita and Steven to Edith's immediately, and Rose had missed her first two weeks of night classes and simply dropped out. Charlie was stunned at her acceptance of the situation, which was not in character for his wife.

" 'To everything there is a season,' " she'd said. "I'd forgotten those words. It seems that now is my season for children, not for education. The subject is closed."

And in the year since, she'd never mentioned college again. But now Charlie had something else for Rose to put her mind on. One look at him in his blue suit would tip off his intelligent wife.

At his normal homecoming time, he pulled in to his garage stall, took the big bank envelope from the seat and walked to the front entrance of the apartment building. A minute later, he was on the third floor. He let himself in the door, stood in the foyer and inhaled the aroma of Rose's cooking. Garlic. His salivary glands went into action. The sound of Steven's babbling competed with the rumble in Charlie's stomach. He heard Susan and Rose talking in the background.

He swung Steven into his arms. "How's my big boy today?"

"Good. I made a fort."

"Is that right?"

The boy nodded. "Mommy didn't like it."

"Uh-oh."

The child turned both palms up in a gesture of bewilderment. "The blankets," he said. "From the beds." But then his eyes gleamed, and he grinned up at his dad. "It was fun."

Charlie got the picture. He tilted his head when he heard Rose's steps. "Sounds like you had some extra work today. A fort, huh?"

"It rained all afternoon so we were busy in the house." Her eyes narrowed as she studied him. "And I see you were busy, too. You went to the bank…"

He nodded.

"…without telling me. If you signed anything, anything at all before talking to me, Charlie Shapiro, I swear I will…I will…well, I don't know what, but I'll be so angry…"

He held up his free hand. "Stop. Everything's filled out, but…I didn't sign yet."

Her slow smile could still dazzle him.

"Thank you, Charlie," she said, and went on before he could answer. "This is a miracle. Are you aware that it's the very first time you've waited to discuss a big decision with me instead of letting me know afterward?"

Well, no, he wasn't aware.

"You bought a car without me," Rose continued. "You decided on this move to the co-op without me. Even the decision to get married was yours. Not that I'm sorry," she added. "But now, finally, it seems that you think I'm an equal partner in this…this life we have?" Her voice rose in question.

She'd blindsided him. He didn't want to talk about their personal relationship. He was prepared for a business discussion—arguments based on finances and risk, questions about location and experience—not statements that knocked him in another direction. He'd get this talk out of the way quickly.

"I've always thought you were an equal partner.

Always." He put Steven down and told him to find Susan, then he reached for his wife. "I love you, Rose. Of course you're equal."

"Love is not the same thing as equal," she replied, resisting his pull. "You can love children, but they don't have equal rights about making family decisions. I'm not a child. My opinion should carry the same weight as yours, even without…without— You know what…"

"I'm dizzy, Rose. I have no idea…" But suddenly, he understood. *Her college degree.* Or lack of it. He put his index finger beneath her chin and raised her face toward him. "My thorny Rose, you are an idiot, and so am I."

He felt her stiffen, but didn't let her go. "I apologize if I've slighted you, but I am not a mind reader. You, who always speak up, why didn't you say something earlier if you felt so insulted?"

"Because I don't spit in the face of a good man. And you are a good man. What right do I have?"

His head hurt. His heart hurt. "Rights, schmites! Can't you give your brain a rest already? Stop thinking so much and just live your life with me. Can't you simply be happy and stop making problems for yourself?"

She snapped her fingers. "*Poof!* I'll be happy. I won't think." She called the children to come to the table. "Looks like everyone's hungry tonight. Let's eat up."

"Start without me," said Charlie.

* * *

When would she ever take things in stride? The depression was over. The war was over. No one else had developed a bundle of nerves like she had. And she trusted Charlie. Really she did.

As she put the dishes away after dinner, she heard water splash from the back of the apartment as he gave Steven a bath. Then came a duet of "Row, Row, Row Your Boat," and she listened to her little son carry a true tune like his dad. Susan joined in to form a trio, and Rose had to wince. Her daughter was *her* daughter. Neither of them would be welcome even in the back row of a chorus. But Charlie never said a word, except last year to Susan's fourth-grade teacher who'd told Susan and another girl only to move their lips when the class was singing.

Oy vey. That was some day. The memory made Rose chuckle now, but no one was laughing when Susan had come home, her chin wobbling, tears behind her eyes, trying to be a big girl about it. The following morning, Charlie was at the school as soon as the doors opened, lecturing on how his daughter's inner spirit was more important than her voice. By the time he was done, Susan was invited to participate.

"Steven's ready for a good-night kiss, Rosie."

She dried her hands and went into her son's room. He was already in bed, smelling deliciously of shampoo and talc. When he saw her, he raised his arms for a hug.

"Hey, my handsome boy." She leaned over and whispered, "I love you, Stevie. No matter what."

"Yup," he said. "'Night." Instantly he was sleeping.

She glanced at Charlie and couldn't contain her snicker. "We lucked out with this one—at least in the sleeping department."

He followed her into the hall where they heard Anita crying. "Now that one," said Rose, stepping toward the master bedroom where they'd set up Anita's crib, "could take some lessons from her big brother. I've got to change her and feed her, Charlie."

"Sure. Feed her in the kitchen where she can visit with her old man."

She nodded. "And we'll talk, Charlie, about the bank loan."

The amount staggered her, but Charlie never blinked. "No guts, no glory," he said.

She wanted guarantees. She couldn't sit still, and as soon as Anita had her fill of rice cereal and banana, Rose put her in her playpen and started pacing the floor, weighing the pros and cons.

"You'll quit at Texaco, invest whatever we have and owe the bank a fortune besides. On the other hand, you'll open with a following. Everyone in the neighborhood knows you now because of your demonstrations on the street—that was smart.

"But I don't want money worries," she continued. "I had that after Joe died. Why take chances when you're making a good salary? Oy vey. I'm driving myself crazy again."

Charlie's lips twitched.

"Stop laughing at me. This is serious."

"The location is great, Rosie. Right on Northern Boulevard, lots of traffic and only five blocks from here. And, if I do say so myself, I'm very good at my job. My reputation in Brooklyn is…" But he started to get uncomfortable, and his face turned pink.

"Sterling," she finished for him. Her Charlie didn't brag. He showed with action. Her heart warmed. He was an honorable man. "You know, your boss might offer a raise for you to stay."

He leaned against the wall. "I've already thought of that."

"What will you say?" she whispered.

"What do you think?" He motioned to the papers spread on the table. "Is this not what we fought for, Rosie? Freedom? Opportunity?" His eyes burned green and gold. They shone with the sincerity of a believer.

She nodded.

"Well, now this dream is in front of me. And I'm hoping very, very hard you'll share it."

Her husband had earned the right to dream, had almost died for that right. Besides which, she trusted him.

She held out her hand. "Count me in."

He swept her into his arms and began dancing them around the floor. "Rosie, Rosie…I already counted you in."

"Well, life's nicer when we're on the same team. Sing a little something so we can have music."

"I made you an officer of the company."

She stumbled. "What?"

"You're going to work, Rose. For C-A-R. Charlie's Auto Repair. Can't do it without you."

June 1954

...and that, Joe, is how I got to be vice president and treasurer of the company, as well as part-time bookkeeper—for which I get paid. Of course, Charlie is president and secretary. We opened for business two months ago, and Charlie already has more work than he can handle. He hired a young mechanic right out of vocational training school because he was too new to have bad habits— Charlie wants to train him the right way. At least, right by Charlie's definition.

There's nothing Charlie can't do with machinery. I understand now why an artillery battalion was the natural fit for him. But why for you?

See you on Susan's next birthday.

Yours forever, Rose

Chapter 8

"**Y**our daughter is an exceptional child, Mrs. Shapiro."

Rose swallowed her smile and leaned back in her chair. Susan's sixth-grade teacher had just uttered the words every parent yearned to hear at an end-of-year conference.

"Thank you," Rose replied. "We think so, too."

"I'm not speaking lightly, Mrs. Shapiro," the teacher said as she opened a folder labeled Susan Rabinowitz—Classwork. She pointed to a book list.

"Susan has read every volume in the class library and half the ones in the school library. You sign her report cards so you know she's a straight-A student. She does more than memorize, Mrs. Shapiro. She can think!"

"We're very proud of her, Mrs. Hingers." Why did the teacher sound so serious?

"If you and Mr. Shapiro agree, I can recommend her skipping a grade in junior high school. Next year she can start in the seventh grade, then jump to the ninth. No eighth grade at all."

She respected Mrs. Hingers's professional opinion, but skipping a whole year of school?

"I'm proud of her," Rose repeated, "but it's a big decision. I'll have to discuss this at home."

"Of course. You should know that there are several students for whom this recommendation will be made. She'd have some familiar faces with her both years."

The teacher reached for an envelope in Susan's folder. "I've hung some of the children's essays on the bulletin board, but not the one in here." She placed the package in Rose's hand. "Father's Day is coming soon, but don't wait to give this to your husband. Tell him he'll need a quiet place to read it."

"All right," said Rose, putting it carefully into her purse. "He'll get it tonight."

Charlie opened the door as soon as the key jingled in her hand. The apartment seemed quiet; he must have put all the children to bed.

"The water's just boiled," he said. "Let's have a cup of tea while you tell me about the school reports."

But Rose didn't wait. She put her purse on the table and spread her arms wide. "We've got two ends of the spectrum, Charlie. Steven's a real *boychick*. The teacher's exhausted from him. He speaks before he thinks. He forgets to raise his hand. But then he makes her laugh, so he gets away with a lot. She told me herself."

"He'll settle down in a while," Charlie said, not bothering to hide his grin or his pride. "He's got personality, Rose. That's what it is."

"Personality? That's what *you* might call it. His teacher is recommending someone stricter for second grade."

Charlie shrugged. "He'll figure her out, too. He likes people, and he wants people to like him. I'm not worried. What about Susan? Solid gold, huh?"

"Like always. But I have something a little special for you. Sit down."

She watched him as he opened the envelope, as he read the essay. From playful to serious, his changing expressions were easy to discern. That was the normal way with Charlie—no secrets. When he looked up, she saw his Adam's apple bob a couple of times as he tried to speak.

Finally he pushed the paper at her. "Read."

She took the composition from him.

June 1, 1955   *Susan Rabinowitz*

The Person I Admire Most

My stepfather's name is Charlie Shapiro, but I call him Dad. He is my dad in every way a daughter could possibly want. He listens. He has patience. He thinks I'm pretty and smart. But most of all, I know he loves me in his heart.

He taught me how to play gin rummy, and he doesn't let me win. But every time I do win, he's happier than if he had taken the hand. We sing together even though I can't carry a tune, and Daddy could sing on Broadway. He just wants us to have a good time together.

I think stepparents have gotten a bad reputation because of fairy tales. There is always a mean stepmother in them so the story could have a villain and not be boring. In real life, it's better to have a stepfather like mine. I love him so much. He's a war hero and a hero to me.

I'm so sorry that my first dad, Joe, had to die in the war. He was a hero, too. But I don't think he could have been a better dad than Mr. Charlie Shapiro.

Rose finished reading and couldn't speak either. She and Charlie had been married almost ten years. Throughout that time, her doubts had come, gone and returned in a cycle of too much thinking, too much worrying. At times, she thought Charlie had come into her life because of some wacky promise he'd made to Joe about "taking care" of Joe's wife. At this moment she didn't care. Marrying Charlie was the best decision she could have made for Susan's sake. Maybe even for her own.

He reached for her hand. "Let's make it official, Rosie. I'd like to adopt her. Give her my name, too."

"That's a mouthful of names," she replied shakily, playing for time.

Charlie nodded. "Yes, indeed. Susan Rabinowitz Shapiro. That is quite a mouthful."

Her mind raced. Her husband was a very good man. A good daddy. Trustworthy. Susan would be better protected legally as Charlie's daughter if anything happened to Rose. And even if he had married her for Joe's sake, Charlie loved Susan as much as he loved his own two children. She couldn't see the negatives, not as she had last year when he wanted to start the business and all Rose saw was debts. No…adoption would provide more security for her daughter.

"All right, Charlie," she replied slowly. "If you really want to…and if Susan's agreeable."

"Fair enough." He sipped his tea, then refolded the essay and gave the envelope to Rose. "File this with the important papers. The very important papers."

Later that evening, she placed the envelope in the Dream Box.

* * *

"Four crack."

"Two dot."

"Flower."

"Mah-jongg," sang out Rose from her seat at the bridge table in her friend's kitchen one evening the following fall. "One-three-five bam and two flowers." She exposed her fourteen tiles on the top of her rack and collected her winnings—appropriately colored chips from the other four women in her group. They'd settle up the cash amount at the end of the night.

She loved the game. As she'd explained to Charlie, "It's like gin rummy but with tiles. There's a measure of luck, but it takes skill and strategy to win. Besides, for one dollar, I get a whole evening's entertainment."

"Forget the sales pitch, Rosie," he'd said. "I know you too well. The truth is, you love to win, even if it's only fifty cents." He'd given her a big kiss and told her to have a good time.

She usually did. And she won often. She, Edith and the friends they'd made in the Heights rotated hosting the game whose popularity was spreading all over the country. They didn't play the original Chinese style, which was a true gambling game, but an Americanized version.

She was having a good time the night she'd made the one-three-five hand. Ten-thirty rolled around quickly, and the evening wrapped up.

"We're going for manicures tomorrow afternoon," said one of the women. "Why don't you join us, Rose."

"Manicures?" She glanced at her nails. "I usually do them myself…when I remember. But I've still got a four-year-old to take care of, so I'll pass. Thanks, though."

"There's a new salon," chimed in another lady. "The owner's really good. And a new dress shop opened on the boulevard a block from your husband's business, Rose."

"I noticed the last time I walked over." She'd actually gone in and browsed, but hadn't bought a thing when she could match the style and supersede the quality herself. One day, when she worked full-time, she'd buy ready-made clothes.

"My Dave says there's nothing Charlie Shapiro doesn't know about cars," continued her friend. "Dave sent two coworkers over, and they had to make appointments. Just like in the beauty parlor! Imagine that a car shop can be so busy."

"Why not?" asked Rose. "Doesn't Dinah Shore sing every Sunday night, 'See the U.S.A. in your Chevrolet'? The economy's booming, and everybody's car crazy. Eventually all the cars need a tune-up, and without an appointment, you can wait for hours."

"I'd wait," said another woman. "Underneath all that grease is one good-looking man." She winked at Rose.

"Underneath all that grease," Rose replied sharply, "is a POW who almost died in Germany along with my first husband. He deserves to work on every car that comes into the shop."

An awkward silence followed, then murmurs of agreement. She felt Edith's hand on her arm and shook her head.

"Sorry, girls." They'd only been making idle chatter about neighborhood growth. "Have fun at the beauty parlor." Rose waved as she let herself out the door with Edith. "Next week at my house."

She and Edith walked to the elevator and pushed the button. Rose felt her shoulders droop. Edith glanced at her, and as soon as the door opened and they were alone inside, she spoke.

"What's wrong, Rosie?"

Rose shook her head. "It's nothing, really. Only...I was never like them, Edith," she said. "They're nice women. Compared to me, they're so happy and lighthearted. They chatter like little parakeets about everyday things, about a bright future. About their wonderful husbands. They never look back. They never worry about anything." She sighed. "I envy them."

The elevator reached the lobby, and Edith opened the door. "I remember when you were happy and lighthearted, Rosie. When you were exactly like them. Don't be so hard on yourself. Their worlds weren't shattered like yours. They didn't lose a husband, a mother and a father. They weren't left alone with a child to care for."

"Or maybe," said Rosie, "they're stronger than I am. They just don't let their worries show, and I do."

Edith shook her head as they walked outside. "But you really don't," she finally said. "Your mind is always on the game."

"Well, I've never learned the art of silly chitchat. Gossip. I like to focus on the mah-jongg tiles. Charlie says..." She paused.

"What? What does Charlie say?"

Rose took a deep breath. "He says I'm afraid of being too happy. That I'm afraid something else will be snatched away."

Her sister stopped walking and turned Rose toward her. "He might be right. You're living a full life, a wonderful life with a husband who adores you, three beautiful children, a growing business..."

But then, Edith became silent and scrutinized Rose. When she spoke again, her voice was sharp. "Or is it Joe who makes you moody? Or feel guilty? Is he still first with you? First in your heart after all this time?"

Rose's stomach cramped. A sharp pain made her gasp. "Oh, God, Edith. I don't know anymore. But maybe, yes...and Charlie knew from the beginning..."

Edith walked toward a streetlamp. "Come here," she said, reaching for her sister and pulling Rose after her. "Answer one question for me."

"What?"

"How's life in the bedroom?"

Rose's skin burned all the way to her eyebrows. Despite her fears, she started to grin.

"Good," Edith said. "So why don't you think about falling in love with your husband?"

But that night, she dreamed about Joe and woke up at three in the morning with tears running down her face. She woke up crying again at four, this time imagining guns pointing at Charlie and of him trudging through the snow. He should have married one of the lighthearted ladies, someone who could harmonize with him in a beautiful duet.

June 1957

Dear Joe,

Just a quick note to tell you that your daughter went to her first formal dance tonight. A graduation dance from junior high. She wore a sweet pale yellow dress with cap sleeves and a full skirt, and the boy she went with gave her a corsage to match. (His mother asked me the color of her dress beforehand.) We took a lot of pictures. I think Charlie and I both got a little farklempt, but we held back the tears until after she left the house.

September 1957

Dear Joe,

Susan started high school today. She's a sophomore now and very excited about not being treated like a baby anymore. She's got a heavy schedule of honors courses, not surprising, and a nice group of friends.

Your daughter has been a joy to raise, Joe.

You'd be very proud of her. She's passionate about what she believes in, sometimes too much so, and her heart breaks. Remember in 1954, when the Supreme Court ordered the integration of schools? When the newsreels came on television and showed the National Guard protecting the Negro children, Susan cried, but she took action. She wrote letters to the governors of at least six southern states.

Charlie's business is going well. I take care of the payroll, receivables, payables and general bookkeeping. But next year, when Anita is in first grade, I'll go to school, too. Charlie doesn't exactly know it yet. I bet he thinks I've given up the idea.

Till the next time,
Yours forever, Rose

She slipped the letter in the manila envelope she now used—the Dream Box not being large enough to hold all of her correspondence—then sat quietly at the desk.

"Joe's letters?" asked Charlie, standing in the doorway of the bedroom.

"Yeah," she said.

"I'll come back." He turned and left the room before she could reply.

As quickly as possible, she placed the envelope on the closet shelf under the Dream Box, then went to find her husband. He stood at the living-room window, gazing at the September night.

"Charlie?" she called softly, walking toward him. "I'm sorry. I put it away. You didn't have to leave the room."

He remained gazing out the window. "His shadow lingers, doesn't it, Rose?"

"Not as much," she whispered.

"We'll be married twelve years next month, and I'm still fighting his ghost."

She wouldn't insult him with a total denial. "Your Rose came with thorns, Charlie, remember? But I tell you, they're getting smaller—and not so sharp."

Suddenly, he began to chuckle. "Dull thorns? Nothing about you is dull, Rosie. I don't know how you do it, but despite everything, you can make me laugh."

"And I love listening to you laugh. You make me feel good, you make everyone feel good." She opened her arms. "Sing to me, Charlie, and let's dance."

Soon, she was leaning against his broad chest, inhaling the familiar aroma of his Old Spice and listening to "her" song in the official translation.

"'Hold me close and hold me fast…'"

For the first time in twelve years, for that one particular moment, Rose was content.

"I'm the oldest person in my day-school class," said Rose in September 1958, "and I don't care." She twirled with her arms outstretched. "I'm very happy. So what if I'm old enough to be everyone's mother!"

"Barely," laughed Charlie. "I love seeing that big smile on your face."

"Ugh," said Steven. "Mom, why are you so excited about being in school? I hate school—too much sitting. I hate everything. And I especially hate Walter O'Malley."

"Who's Walter O'Malley?" asked Rose, focusing on her son. "Did you get into a fight?"

Her nine-year-old stared at her as though she were speaking Hungarian, then turned to his father. "Doesn't she know, Dad? Doesn't she remember?" he asked, his voice pained.

"Know what?" She grabbed Charlie's wrist. "What's going on? Is Steven in trouble?"

But Charlie couldn't answer. His eyes were shining, his free hand covered his mouth—and then he burst out laughing.

"Steven's right, Rosie. Walter O'Malley is evil. He moved our boys to Los Angeles. No more games at Ebbets Field. The Brooklyn Dodgers are gone from Brooklyn."

Ah, on safer ground. "But…but wasn't that last year?"

Charlie nodded. "We're still in shock. A whole summer without a Dodgers game." He hooked his arm around Steven's neck. "We miss them."

Charlie had taken the kids to Ebbets Field many times during the past couple of years, but it was Steven who lived, breathed, despaired or cheered every play. It was Steven who'd memorized the lineup, the batting averages and who couldn't wait to grow up and play for the Dodgers.

"Well, can't you go to a Yankees game?" asked Rose, trying to find a logical answer.

Steven's groan came long and low. She thought he might actually cry.

"Mom! Gil Hodges plays for the Dodgers. And Pee Wee Reese and Duke Snider. They're our team!"

She rolled her eyes and glanced at Charlie. "You handle this one."

"Okay, I will." Charlie looked at Steven. "How'd you like to take a trip across the country and see the Dodgers play in L.A. next season?"

Her husband had lost his mind. Rose was about to protest, when she saw her son's face. Joy, elation, admiration were written all over it. His dad could do anything. And Charlie's face? Total enchantment. Total love for the child they had created together.

"Charlie?" she whispered, her mind racing through the logistics. They could afford it. She'd just started working part-time in the neighborhood dress shop, and Charlie's business was, thank God, very sound. Her responsibilities there were part-time, as well.

"Shh. It's all right. I'm making memories, Rose. He'll never forget it."

Steven turned to her then, a question on his face.

"Come here, Stevie." She put her hands on his shoulders and bent lower. "You'll be a good boy? You won't let go of Daddy's hand in the stadium? There'll be thousands of people there."

He nodded. "I'm not a baby, Mom. I didn't get lost at Ebbets Field."

He'd memorized the Brooklyn ballpark. "Okay. But here's the deal. To earn this trip, which is expensive, you have to do something for me. And you have to do it all by yourself."

Her son glanced at his dad. Charlie shrugged.

Rose said, "I want you to write a detailed composition about how Jackie Robinson got to play for the Dodgers. What happened? Who was involved? Where was he playing before he got to Brooklyn? Use a dictionary to spell words you don't know.

"And when you finish that, I want to see your own calculations of the current roster's batting averages as well as the averages of the players on the team they play in Los Angeles."

She'd kept her son's attention so far. This type of request was something new. "I'm tired, Steven, of hearing the teachers say you can do better, that you don't try. I want to see you do your best—and without any help from Susan."

Rose put out her hand. "Do we have a deal?"

A slow smile traveled across his face. "It's a piece of cake, Mom." He put his hand in hers and they shook.

The next afternoon, Steven arrived home with three books from the school library about Jackie Robinson. He didn't look happy.

"You know what the teacher said, Mom?"

"No, sweetheart. I wasn't there."

"She said it was about time I turned into Susan's brother."

Oops. Rose could anticipate where this conversation was leading. "What did you say?"

"I told her I already am Susan's brother."

Rose beamed at him. "Perfect answer, Steve. Excellent, in fact."

He flashed her a quick grin. "But I knew what she really meant, Mom. All the teachers remember Susan. I still hate school."

Rose pulled the boy into her arms. "Listen to me, Steven, and remember what I say. You are you, and Susan is Susan. Your job is to be the best Steven Joel Shapiro you can be. That's it. You're my wonderful boy, and I love you."

Steven was his father's child—sensitive, passionate and loving. Each child was unique. She would visit his teacher and explain that to her before Charlie caught on and stormed the school again.

That winter, Charlie didn't know whether his shop was busier than his family or vice versa. With Rose in college and Susan a high-school junior, and Steven having homework each day, his house had turned into a study hall. The kitchen and dining-room tables were usually covered with textbooks, notebooks, reference books, an assortment of pencils and pens and Anita's art projects. His youngest daughter insisted on doing "homework", too. He found Rose's texts on the living-room couch—her most comfortable spot. Of course, sometimes she was so comfortable, she fell asleep.

He expected this particular December night to be no different. He turned his key in the lock and opened the door. The dining-room table was set for dinner with their Hanukkah menorah in the center, candles waiting to be lit. The aroma of Rose's extensive cooking, which he hadn't enjoyed in months, came rushing to his nostrils, and his stomach rumbled.

And there was Rose, her brown, curly hair softly framing her face, her smile spontaneous when she greeted him. His heartbeat quickened.

"Daddy's home," she called out over her shoulder as she approached.

Up close, he saw dots of perspiration on her forehead. He kissed her and said, "You're working too hard, but it smells delicious."

"Cooking's a pleasure, even the potato latkes. The other stuff..." She shrugged.

The children bustled in with stories of their day, more excited than usual because of the first night of the holiday, and he couldn't follow up with a question.

Hanukkah had crept up on him. He'd forgotten the exact night—it changed every year because of the lunar calendar—but as he looked at the family assembled at the table, at Rose lighting the candles, and heard everyone join in with the blessing, he thought, *This is another memory.*

"Don't move," he said. "I'm getting the camera."

Moans and groans around the table. "Eat up," he continued. "I'll snap you with your mouths full."

"Oh, Charlie..." Rose shook her head, but she was smiling.

Brisket, potato latkes, applesauce—everyone was digging in. "What's on your mind, Rosie?" he asked.

Susan answered for her mother. "Final exams. She's a nervous wreck."

"To be perfectly honest," began Rose, "I liked Shakespeare better when Joe told the stories. As far as I'm concerned, Romeo and Juliet were two spoiled teenagers, and..."

But Charlie didn't hear a word after Joe's name, a first at the dinner table. Finally he said, "Joe was a great storyteller. He could entertain fifty men like nobody else."

"I like stories, Daddy," said six-year-old Anita. "Maybe Joe could tell me a story."

"Oh, brother!" Steven said. "Don't you know anything? Joe can't tell you a story. He's dead. He's Susan's father who died in the war. Don't you remember?"

Charlie glanced at Rose, but her attention was on Susan. Susan, Joe's natural daughter, who was now sitting very quietly, totally unlike her usual self. He had to reach her.

"Your Daddy Joe was a hero, Susie," began Charlie, "and he was my friend. A very good man." Immediately the words echoed in his ears. They were the same words Rose used to describe him, and he clenched his fist. *A very good man.* Perfect words to describe a friend. Was that it? Was that all he'd ever be to Rose?

Later. He'd think about it later. Susan needed him.

"I know he was a hero," Susan said, but her mouth was tight, her complexion pale. "War is stupid!" she burst out. "It's not fair that he died."

His daughter was fifteen going on sixteen next month, as she liked to say, and her reaction seemed totally appropriate. At least, Charlie thought so.

"Fair?" he replied. "There's no such thing as fair, honey. Not in war. And sometimes not in life." He wouldn't mention love, but he felt Rose's gaze on him.

"Daddy was a hero, too," said Rose. "Remember I told you about how he was captured?"

Tears formed in his daughter's eyes. "That must have been horrible."

Charlie shrugged. "It was wartime, sweetheart. It's over."

Susan shook her head. "It'll never be over. Never. Not as long as one country wants what another country has."

Charlie stared at her. "Where did you learn this?"

She shrugged. "In school. And, you know, I read—a lot. It's depressing."

"Not if the good guys win," Steven replied.

"It doesn't matter, " said Susan. "War will break out again and that's what's depressing. Someday I'm going to figure out what to do about it."

"You're going to figure out how to stop war?" Rose asked, looking as confused and worried as Charlie felt.

"Yes," said Susan. "Why not? Maybe it has to do with leadership... Daddy, why were your lines stretched so thin in the Ardennes Forest?"

"Why were...?" He stopped, memories swirling as quickly as the snow had swirled around him that day. "Well, the brass thought it was the least likely spot for an enemy offensive because the roads in the heavy forest were too narrow for a mechanized division to move through."

"They were wrong," Susan whispered.

He was back there again, after so many years. Back in the snow and freezing cold. Back with Joe, noting his surprise at the strength of the onslaught. Charlie saw his pal clearly, as clearly as on the day he'd died, saw him running from man to man, ignoring the snow, yelling directives, yelling encouragement and then...then he saw him jerk back and fly into the air after he was hit, the shock on his face.

Other men burst into his mind's eye, men they'd lost: Bobby Truman from Mississippi, George Estafani from Queens, Vic DiLillo from Jersey. One by one they kept coming, crowding his brain.

"Excuse me," said Charlie, mopping the sweat from his face. "I need to take a walk."

"Not without me," said Rose. "I'll just grab my coat."

He reached for the doorknob. "Stay with the children, Rose. I'd rather be alone."

Chapter 9

He'd rather be alone? Not acceptable. Charlie left the apartment, but Rose grabbed her coat and ran down the three flights of stairs to the lobby. She knew her husband would never have had the patience to wait for an elevator, not when he needed to walk.

Charlie always seemed to disappear in the middle of an important discussion. Whenever he was troubled about something, he walked. Whenever he had a decision to make, he walked—alone. But not this time.

The lobby was empty. She raced into the cold night air and spotted him almost at the corner. The man had covered lots of ground. She called his name, and he turned immediately. Although he waited for her, he didn't look happy.

"Go upstairs, Rose. I need to set a fast pace."

"You think I'm too old to keep up?" She quickened her step. "What are you thinking?"

He sighed. "I'm thinking that I'm a grown man, and I don't need an escort."

She waved that away. "Pish, tush. That doesn't count."

"Rose, for crying out loud. Here's the truth. I'm thinking that if I was alone I wouldn't have to make conversation. Go home."

"No. I'll be quiet."

His raised brow was his only response. To be fair, she couldn't blame him—they both knew she wasn't the silent type. She didn't like secrets; she didn't like brooding. When she detected a problem in the family, she probed hard, and she didn't let go until the matter was resolved—to her satisfaction. This time, however, she'd keep her jaws clenched if it killed her.

It almost did. The frigid air invading her lungs made her chest tight. She wrapped a scarf around her head and mouth to warm the air she breathed, but she couldn't keep up with Charlie. Finally, she dashed forward five steps, tapped him on the shoulder and motioned that she'd go back.

"Too cold for you?"

She shook her head. "Can't breathe," she whispered.

His eyes widened, and he twisted her scarf more securely, then put his arm around her. Together, they slowly returned to their building. They stayed in the lobby until Rose's labored breathing returned to normal.

She glared at him. "You're safe in winter."

Suddenly he started one of his belly laughs. "That's my Rosie," he began. "You can't breathe, you're choking, but you stick to your mission. You're one in a million, Rose, and I love you. Very, very much."

She stroked his cheek. "Charlie, Charlie…you are such a good man." She kissed him.

"Wow," he said afterward. "I think it's time we went upstairs on a date."

She felt herself get excited at the suggestion. Thank God that part of their marriage contained no secrets. But the war still haunted him. Susan's questions had triggered this walk in the cold night. After so many years, Charlie still had memories he couldn't shake. Or was it only the memory of Joe that haunted them both?

Board of Education, City of New York
June 1960
Graduation Program

1. *Processional*
2. *Welcome, Principal John C. Arnold*
3. *Salutatorian's Address, Paul J. Grossman*
4. *Selections by Orchestra, Conductor Rick Woods*
5. *Keynote Address, Honorable Robert F. Wagner, Mayor, New York City*
6. *Valedictorian's Address, Susan R. Shapiro*

Susan's high-school graduation would be held outdoors to accommodate the twelve hundred students in the senior class. Forest Park had a permanent band shell and row upon row of benches would be installed for the event.

In her bedroom, Rose glanced critically at Anita and Steven, straightening her son's tie, brushing her younger daughter's bangs, as they all got ready to leave the apartment.

"If Susan wasn't such a brain, we wouldn't have to go to this thing," complained eleven-year-old Steven. "I could be playing baseball with my friends."

"So don't go." Susan walked into the room and looked at her siblings. "I didn't ask you to. In fact, I don't want to go myself."

Rose glanced at her daughter. "What's wrong?"

"My freedom of speech is being usurped." From her straight back to her pursed mouth to her gleaming eyes, Susan was defending her principles. They'd been through this type of situation before.

"Oh, for goodness' sake..." sighed Rose. "Now what?"

"Forget it. Maybe I won't speak at all. I'll let Paul Grossman have all the glory." Her daughter glided out of the room. "Dad?" she called.

Good. Let Charlie handle her today. As for Paul... The boy was both Susan's nemesis and her best friend. Only a half point behind Susan's overall grade-point average and Susan's co-captain on the debating team, Paul Grossman would be attending

Columbia University in the fall on a full scholarship, just like Susan. Susan would go to Barnard, the women's college, while Paul attended the all-male Columbia College. They'd be a block apart in the upper Manhattan area called Morningside Heights.

"Is Susan in trouble?" asked Anita.

Her brother answered. "Nope. But she will be. Right, Mom? Don't you always say that she makes trouble for herself?"

"Only in the past two years. Before that, she was the perfect child. Just like you!"

Steven grinned up at his mother, and Rose laughed. Her son knew his track record. It wasn't perfect, but it wasn't too bad, either. He was a happy child who would soon start preparing for his bar mitzvah, the boy-to-man rite of passage for every Jewish male. In the modern world, Rose thought, a thirteen-year-old remained a boy even after the big event and despite the certain privileges he earned in the synagogue, but she had no objections to the tradition. Rose only hoped the studying got the kid to think about something more than baseball.

A high-school graduation was also a rite of passage, and now Rose ushered her younger two into the living room where Susan and Charlie were talking.

"Your speech is political, Susie. Very one-sided. A graduation speech isn't a debate. No wonder your adviser wants you to change it."

"Paul said the same thing, but, Dad—"

Charlie held up his hand. "Think a minute. You're addressing a broad audience, not just a segment of people who think the way you do. You've got to figure out how to get all of them to listen without insulting them."

"That sounds reasonable," said Rose.

"As soon as you mention Kennedy's name, the Nixon supporters will tune you out. Is that what you want?"

But Susan didn't want to let go of her passion, the fight for her ideals. Rose studied the interesting mix of expressions crossing her daughter's face until the girl finally murmured, "The bigger picture. You want me to address the bigger picture, which is…?"

"Getting out to vote," said Rose. "Everybody's vote counts in a democracy."

"Bingo," said Charlie. "All you have to do is change the slant. Getting people involved in the process is what you want."

"You mean, it's what I'll settle for…but, yes. I can do this. Thanks." She scribbled onto the pages of her speech. "Okay. I'm ready. Just need the cap and gown." She quickly left the room.

Rose and Charlie looked at each other. "Another crisis averted?" she asked.

Charlie shrugged. "We can only hope. Notice that Paul's advice wasn't enough? She still came to us."

"I hope she never stops," Rose said. "In the fall, she'll be a college girl. Her world will be bigger than her parents'…"

Steven spoke next. "Aren't you glad Anita and I aren't brainiacs?"

"Your brain works pretty darn well," Rose replied.

Steven shook his head. "Not like hers, but who cares? I have more fun. Susan always studies or she's on the phone with Paul arguing with him. What kind of a girl is she?"

"I *love* Susan," said Anita. "Except that she's your favorite, isn't she, Mommy?"

Oh, good Lord, had she heard right? Who knew Anita harbored such thoughts? Rose bent closer to her younger daughter. "What makes you say something like that, Anita, when I love you all so much with my whole heart?"

"Well, Susan gets to stay up late, and you and Daddy talk to her more and you go shopping with her. My friends go shopping with their moms—they're always showing off their new stuff—but you always sew mine. And Susan can do whatever she wants. I never get to do anything!"

"Mom, don't listen to her," Steven said before turning to his little sister. "Susan's seventeen and a half. You're eight. What do you expect? You're just a baby."

"No, I'm not."

"Yes, you are."

"Hold it!" said Charlie.

Both children stared at him.

"It's time to leave."

"Anita," Rose said, not quite able to dismiss

her child's comment. "Who's my favorite eight-year-old?"

"Me!"

"Come here." She opened her arms, and her baby threw herself into them. "Okay, *mamele*. That's better. Now we can go."

Their seats were reserved near the front, close to the stage, because of Susan's part in the program. It took them a while to get there, though, because Charlie had to greet at least a hundred people—half of whom he didn't know! Her husband had never met a stranger, which was why his business thrived. And why they had so many friends.

She did, however, recognize Paul Grossman's parents and greeted them with enthusiasm. "I hope, Doris, that I'm not the only mother with butterflies in her stomach."

Doris Grossman laughed nervously and patted her waist. "I'm with you all the way." The woman looked toward the stage. "I could never do it."

"Funny how they both thrive on public speaking."

Paul's father joined in. "It's because they relish the argument and don't care at all about who's listening."

"Which is why Susan had to change her speech. The administration cared who was listening." Rose reached for Charlie's hand. "I'm nervous. She might…might still do what she wants. Can they withhold her diploma? Withdraw the scholarship?"

"Borrowing trouble again, Rose?" Charlie gave her a quick hug. "She'll be fine."

Paul's speech focused on improving the world by striving for excellence in the graduates' personal and professional lives. Being dedicated to doing their best would make a difference for everyone.

Rose nodded. A good, safe speech with a point that each youngster could understand. Now, if only Susan couched hers the same way...

She almost did. Almost. Her talk about responsible citizenship and voting was perfect until she added a postscript before leaving the podium:

"Although I'm not old enough to vote in the upcoming election, I'll be doing my part this summer by volunteering in the campaign of John F. Kennedy for president of the United States. The headquarters are nearby, so, come join me and make a difference!"

"Oh, no! She endorsed him. After all our talking..."

But the applause drowned out her thoughts. She glanced at the stage. Susan held up her hand.

"Let me add that Nixon's headquarters are nearby also. Volunteer, then, get out and vote. Thank you."

The applause was thunderous at this point. Rose glanced at Charlie who was on his feet, eyes bright with tears. "That is some kid. She's got it all."

Joe would be kvelling.

Charlie turned to her then. "I wish Joe could see this."

Startled at the similarity of their thoughts, she replied, "Who knows? Maybe he does."

She glanced at her younger children. If Joe were still alive, there would be no Steven or Anita. Instinctively, Rose reached for her son's hand, then her daughter's and squeezed them gently.

"What do you think?" she asked.

Steven sighed. "Like I said before, she's a brain."

"Mommy, is Susan the smartest person in the world?" asked Anita. "Everybody's clapping for her."

"Not in the world, Anita, but she's pretty good for seventeen. And almost a half."

That evening, Rose placed the graduation program into the Dream Box. Across the back of the booklet, she wrote, *Your daughter made us all proud. She's a thinker with your imagination. She has your way with words. Rose.*

She closed the box and put it away on the closet shelf. No letter tonight.

Charlie had learned to leave Rose alone in the evening on those days when Susan was the focus of activities. He didn't want to see his wife reading Joe's letters, and *she* didn't want him to see her. Every time he'd shown up unexpectedly, he'd startled her and made her uncomfortable.

Who knew how a woman's mind worked? Did she think she had two husbands? That she was being held accountable by two? Sure, he wouldn't want Joe to be forgotten, especially for Susan's sake, but it was Rose who kept him vitally alive.

On the night of Susan's high-school graduation,

he read the newspaper in the living room, then planned to take a long walk until he was sure the Dream Box was packed away again. It was safer if he didn't know the truth, didn't know where Rose's heart really lay.

Of course, he already knew the answer—way down deep inside. Charlie was her friend. He couldn't blame his wife if he was second best; she'd warned him. His own mother had warned him. And after fifteen years of marriage, he had to admit to himself that they'd been right.

He'd always be second best. Sharing a life wasn't enough to change that. Sharing the laughter, tears and children they'd produced together didn't alter his status. As for sharing a marriage bed…well, he had no complaints there, but what did that mean? Was being a delightful partner her way of repaying him for "saving" her and Susan? If, just once, he'd heard an "I love you" from her… But he hadn't. Not even in the throes of their lovemaking. Not even when he sprinkled her with kisses and words of love.

Without Rose's heart, he'd always be second best.

He had a good life. In fact, most people would envy him. But he wanted more. He wanted to be first.

So, on the night Susan graduated, after he'd finished reading the paper, when Rose was busy with the Dream Box—busy with her first husband— Charlie went for a walk. A very long one.

* * *

"It's almost eleven o'clock, Charlie. Where were you? I was ready to call the cops."

"You know I like to take the night air," he replied.

"Yes," Rose said, "when you have something on your mind. But today was a happy day. What's wrong?" She knew her husband. His expression was set. His hazel eyes dark. Something was bothering him.

"Time is passing, Rose. The kids are growing up," he said. "They don't require as much attention…I mean, physically. No diapers. No crying babies. We all sleep well at night."

She nodded in agreement, but she saw that he wasn't finished, and became uneasy.

"You're busy with your schoolwork and—" he waved his arm "—the household and the dress shop."

"And the bookkeeping for the business," she added quickly. Where was he going with this?

"True," he said. "But not for long."

A chill raced through her, and she shivered. "Not for long? You're scaring me, Charlie. What are you talking about?"

"I'm going to expand, Rosie. Open more repair shops. I'll be hiring a full-time bookkeeper when I do, so you won't have to worry about it anymore. You can finally concentrate on your own education and career."

"I've been managing," she began, "and I'm graduating next year." She paused to study him. "This isn't open for discussion, is it?" she asked quietly. "I can see on your face that you've made this decision. The same way you decided things in the beginning."

He nodded. "That's right. The subject is closed. I'm going to do it."

Anger roared, then fear consumed her. Her legs felt like jelly, and her stomach rolled. "Out of the blue...? Like that?" She snapped her fingers.

He remained silent for a long minute. "The timing may be sudden, but the thought has been hovering in the back of my mind. I need to see how far I can go."

"But why? You've already proven yourself. CAR, Inc., is solid. Even a worrier like me can see that. It's doing well all because of you."

"Then three shops will do three times as well. I'm working up a five-year plan and then I'll go to the bank."

Rose heaved herself to her feet, bewildered. "I don't understand. You're not a greedy man. You don't even look happy about this decision." She shook her head. "I just don't know what to say."

"I know you don't," Charlie replied quietly. "So don't say anything at all."

Long Island, 2007

"Those were tough days," said Rose, rooting around in the Dream Box. Finally she pulled out the cover to the graduation program. "Look, Susan. You and Paul are both listed right there."

Susan reached for the program. "I remember

that day very well. It may sound funny now, but I thought that was my last day of childhood. I was a true adult that summer—especially when I went off to college in the fall."

"They were busy years," said Charlie.

"A happy time for me," said Susan. "I loved those first years at school. So did Paul, not that we were together every minute."

"Oh, come on," said Rose. "You and Paul were inseparable from the beginning."

Susan giggled, glanced at her husband, then looked at Rose. "Did you know, Mom, that at the start of every year, Paul and I decided we had to date five other people just to keep ourselves honest."

"What?"

Susan leaned against the back of her chair. "It was ridiculous. Whenever he had a meal with someone else, he'd report back to me the next day and check a number off the list. One down, four to go."

"And you?" asked Rose. "Did you do the same thing?"

"I was worse. I didn't even want to go out with anyone else. We were really ridiculous," she repeated with a chuckle.

"Lizzy and Matt are like you and Paul were," said Rose. "They have eyes only for each other."

Susan's laughter stopped. "I wish…" She jumped from her seat, hands fisted, anger radiating from every pore. "Damn it!" She whirled and leaned against the counter, her hands behind her back, holding on as she faced her family. "I've spent my life trying to make a difference, and…and for what? Our kids still go off to fight."

"Look at her!" said Charlie. "Just like she was at seventeen. Nothing's changed. She's still full of piss and vinegar."

"But I've failed!"

"No, no," said Charlie immediately. "You haven't failed. You've succeeded, more than you realize. Your books, your radio show…they make people talk. They make people think. That's your job, and you've done very, very well. As for our Matthew, well, he has to make his own decision."

Susan frowned. "Maybe. I'm not sure. I'm not seeing clearly right now. It's hard being a mother. It was easier being a kid and sure we had all the answers. Remember, Dad, when we marched on Washington in the summer of '63? When Martin Luther King gave his 'I Have a Dream' speech?"

"Sure I remember. Your mother wouldn't let you go, even with Paul, unless I went, too."

Susan looked at her mother. "You were afraid of the crowds?"

Rose shrugged. "One young girl among tens of thousands—no, hundreds of thousands of people? You said it yourself, it's hard being a mother. You protect your children especially when they have no fear. I didn't know that event would wind up to be such a peaceful rally." She reached for Susan's hand.

"I would have gone also, Susie Q, but I was working then. My first full-time job in public accounting."

"I remember you wanted to graduate before I did," laughed Susan. "That was your goal...you always had goals, but none exceeded earning that college diploma."

Rose slapped the table. "And I did it! I was forty-two, the oldest graduate in the class of '62."

"But the cutest," said Charlie. "Always was adorable."

"No wonder you two have lasted sixty years!" said Paul. "Dad can throw a great compliment."

Rose chuckled. "Now he says I was adorable, but he barely noticed me in the early sixties. He was so busy growing the business and fending off some...some harlots!"

Susan burst out laughing. "Harlots? Who uses that word anymore? And Dad? No way. Besides, today is a day to celebrate, not dredge up ancient history."

But Rose foraged in the Dream Box once more and pulled out a bank-loan agreement. She tilted her head and stared at her husband. "Remember this piece of ancient history?"

Susan stared at the paper. It was dated January 20, 1961—her eighteenth birthday. The amount of the loan staggered her.

There'd been no family party that year...

Charlie wasted no time putting his plan into action. That summer after Susan's graduation, he scouted sites for his new locations. Queens was still a bustling place, and he traveled the borough to find the right spot, one that was convenient for customers, convenient and affordable for him.

Then he looked east toward booming Long Island. Young couples were leaving the city and buying their own homes there. Like Aaron and Maddie had done several years earlier. They wanted space and privacy, backyards for their kids and no neighbors sharing a wall.

The majority of young couples, however, were living house poor. Their big purchase took every dollar they had, and they'd probably try to fix their cars themselves first before paying someone else to do it. So Charlie focused on the established towns, where financial success could be seen in the brick Tudors, tennis courts and pools.

He drove up and down Northern Boulevard, which continued from his own home to Great Neck, Manhasset, Roslyn—populated towns on the north shore of Long Island that still had room to grow.

By summer's end, he'd targeted two locations, one in Bayside, Queens, and one in Great Neck. He put down binders on the land.

He spent the fall evenings preparing a five-year business plan to present to the bank. But first he showed it to Rose. Or tried to.

She was lounging on the couch reading the *Wall Street Journal* and watching the news at the same time. That was Rose. Always had to accomplish two or three things at once.

He pulled the last piece of paper from the Royal portable typewriter they'd bought years ago and announced, "It's done."

She barely raised an eyebrow over the newspaper. "That's nice." She looked back to the paper.

"I'd like you to read it."

"It's been your baby from the beginning, Charlie. I don't think so."

"That's it? You're not going to ask twenty thousand questions about the debt and payback and interest rates. You're not going to wonder where our next meal is coming from?" This was extremely unusual for Rose. She always worried about money.

"I don't have to ask questions. I'm graduating in a few months, and I've already got job offers at two accounting firms. We won't go hungry no matter what happens."

Clearly finished talking, she went back to her damn newspaper. He clipped his pages together and placed them in the center of the kitchen table. His accountant had worked up the financials with him, so Charlie was confident of the figures—the projected ones and the amount to request from the bank. It wasn't that he needed Rose's input, he wanted it. Regardless of his intentions, taking such a big step felt uncomfortable without her.

"I'm going out," he said, walking toward the door.

She nodded. "I figured. Take a scarf. It's November."

She talked to him like he was five years old. "There's something you should know."

Finally he'd gotten her attention. "You're still listed as vice president and treasurer," he said as he closed the door behind him.

When he returned, he found her note:

Charlie, this is an ambitious plan with much risk, but I think you'll succeed. Please see my suggestions below. I will remain treasurer on the condition that your bookkeeper now report to me in person every month. I will not lend my professional name blindly to any enterprise—even yours. R.

"No problem," he murmured. His eyes jumped back to four words: *I think you'll succeed.* He read them over and over, knowing her praise reflected only her business judgment, but he tucked the comments deep inside himself anyway. Still reaching for scraps from the woman he loved. He swallowed hard. For the first time since the POW camp, he wanted to punch someone; he wanted to bash and pound until the sucker lay in a bloody heap without moving.

When the loan came through on Susan's birthday, Charlie shifted into overdrive to triple the size of his business. Like Rose, he was forty-one years old. In the prime of his life.

Chapter 10

Two months prior to the bar mitzvah, Rose sat at the dining-room table, the box of invitations in front of her. She stared at the guest list, shook her head, then glanced into the living room where Charlie watched television.

"Who are these people, Charlie? I've never heard of them." She rattled off three names.

"From the bank."

"The bank? Since when do we invite bankers to a bar mitzvah?"

"Since I've gone from grease monkey to business-man."

Rose's eyes narrowed. She herself had never used the term or even thought of Charlie as a grease monkey, but she understood what he meant.

"I know you make friends easily, but that's a lot of extra people at twenty-five dollars a plate."

"Worth every penny."

She shook her head and continued reading his list. John Sawyer owned a chain of dry cleaners that delivered to people's homes, and Charlie had the contract to repair his trucks. Then there was Bill Olson who owned Grandma's Old-Fashioned Bakery. Charlie maintained his fleet of vehicles, too.

"My goodness..." Her voice sounded rusty. "Is there anyone you left out?"

"It's all about marketing and customer relations," replied Charlie. "I did some research and went after the accounts—but you know that, you've seen the books. And now I want to show my appreciation—provide a personal touch."

She wasn't going to argue. "I'm just happy you got the accounts."

Of course, she'd noticed some external changes. His hands were cleaner, he didn't have to use special soaps and solvents as often to get good results, and he'd also bought two new suits, a sport jacket and new slacks.

"You're not working on cars anymore, are you?"

"Sometimes I do to keep up-to-date. The men have to know they can trust my advice."

The men. He'd hired and fired until he'd staffed the two new stores with people he liked and who had the instinct he had for engines. She picked up the guest list again.

"Besides the money people, you've got two tables for your staff. Charlie, half the total guests at the party are business associates, not family."

"So what? A party's a great time to strengthen relationships." Suddenly he paused. He stared at her and quietly said, "Aren't you planning on asking your boss? Or your close associates at your accounting firm?"

"No," she said. "Even though I'm studying for the CPA exam, I'm still a lowly auditor— No one would bother to attend. Besides, I like to separate my business from my personal life."

"Are you sure about that?" Charlie continued, a smile now in his voice. "After your wonderful raise and evaluation? The partners didn't reward everyone with an increase like yours, Rosie. They're crazy about you."

She felt herself blush at the compliment, and when she glanced at Charlie, she burned hotter yet. When his hazel eyes darkened but still glowed with warmth, when he tilted his head a certain way as he was doing now...the way he used to... She knew that look well.

Her hands fluttered, and she placed them in her lap. She whispered, "What?"

Charlie approached her. "It's been a long time..."

She thought quickly—they'd had relations last weekend. She began to shake her head.

"...between dances." Charlie held out his hand to her. For a split second, she believed she saw a flicker of doubt in his eyes, but then she didn't think at all. She simply stood and walked into his arms.

He began to hum...not "her" song but a Frank Sinatra tune instead. Rather than feel romantic, she realized she hadn't often felt "young at heart" through the years. A sadness swept through her, but she continued dancing while Charlie sang a song about hope and fancy.

When he stopped, she said, "You were right. It's been a long time. And I've missed it."

All the tasks and stress of planning for Steven's big day flew out of Rose's mind when she saw her son in front of the temple's sanctuary, leading the congregation in prayer. He chanted his Torah and *haftarah* portions in a clear, boyish voice, every word sung on key. He truly was his father's son.

Family, friends and Charlie's business associates

almost filled the room. Susan had brought Paul.
They both had jobs that summer that actually paid
a salary. "About time," Charlie had said with a grin.

Now Rose was content to watch her son. He
seemed confident up there in front of the large
group. Despite his earlier grumbling, he'd studied
hard—probably afraid to make a fool of himself—
and it was paying off.

She smiled happily at him until she realized what
would come next: his speech. Steven's personal
speech. She squeezed Charlie's hand.

"Have you read it?" she whispered.

"Nope."

"Neither have I. Oy vey. How did it slip by me?"

"Relax. His teacher has it under control. Besides,
he's our kid. He'll be fine."

"But will I be?" She sat back and listened, and
enjoyed how Steven personalized the standard
thank-yous to his teachers and rabbis. Then he
turned toward her and his father.

"This part's for you guys."

She didn't know what to expect and held her breath.

"If every kid could have Rose and Charlie
Shapiro as parents, we'd have a better world, a
happier place. So I feel special.

"My dad believes in making memories. One of
my best was going with him to see the Dodgers
play ball. And I'm not just talking about at Ebbett's
Field. My dad actually took me to a game in Los
Angeles the year after our team left town because I

thought the world was coming to an end. Of course, I was only nine—" he smiled "—but how many dads would do that?"

Steven looked directly at Charlie. "Thanks, Dad. You made a memory I'll never forget."

Rose thought her hand would break from Charlie squeezing so hard. So much for his cavalier attitude.

"I used to hate school," her son continued. "Frankly, I'd still rather play ball, but my mom never, ever lost her patience with me when she helped me with my homework. She never yelled. She never got mad. She just explained stuff and made it seem easy. She always believed I could do it. And I did. Now junior high's not so bad. In fact, I had a great year. It was even fun. So thank you, Mom, for not giving up on me."

Rose's tears gushed, making her mascara run, and she couldn't find a tissue.

"Here," said Charlie, offering his handkerchief. "You deserve it."

"I guess I've done my job," said Steven into the microphone. "They're both crying. That's why I only get mushy every thirteen years."

"A comedian, too," Charlie murmured.

"It was worth every penny, every aggravation, putting this day together," said Rose.

"You and I," began Charlie, "we made a pretty neat boy."

There was something in his voice…an emphasis

when he said, *you and I.* Instantly she understood. You and I...and *not* Joe. She knew it as if he'd said the words out loud.

She threaded her fingers through his. "We've made *two* neat kids."

And nothing would change that fact. Not even their roller-coaster relationship.

June 22, 1962

Dear Joe,

It's Saturday afternoon. Charlie is at one of the new shops, and Steven and Anita are at the movies. I'm writing to you when I'm alone because Charlie doesn't like seeing me with the Dream Box. I don't want to confront him because he might say something I don't want to hear. Something about you or about the letters. I won't stop writing to you or reading your letters from time to time and I won't throw out the Dream Box, so I think it's best to do it in private.

Your namesake did a great job last Saturday at his bar mitzvah. Your family came. Your parents are Grandma and Grandpa to Steven and Anita, just as they are to Susan. They like the "honor," I think. Your dear sister and Lenny have no children, so my three are it. I will tell you honestly, Joe, that your parents have aged too quickly, and they carry an air of resignation about them.

Charlie's parents, on the other hand... Tessie doesn't know what quiet means, but she's gracious with your mother, and that's what counts. Tessie doesn't believe in getting older, only better, she says.

Rose twirled her pen while she considered what she wanted to say next. Through the years, the writing had helped her to figure things out. She hoped it would help now.

Charlie is working hard. The three shops take up all his time and I hardly see him, not even at dinner on many days. He seems to be on a crusade to grow, grow, grow. Yesterday I asked if he was getting greedy in his middle age. He laughed, but it didn't sound humorous.

"It's not about the money, Rose," he said. "It's about the achievement."

"But if you drop dead from the achievement, it will all be for nothing," I told him.

All he said was, "Don't worry. You'll have a lot of insurance this time." Then he walked out of the room.

I couldn't have uttered another word at that moment anyway.

At her desk, Rose thought back to the day before.

How she'd run after Charlie when she'd collected herself. How she'd attacked him.

"Why are you talking that way, Charlie?" she'd asked. "What's the matter with you? You heard Steven's speech—he adores you! You want the kids not to have a father? What about Anita? What about Susan? Even college girls need their dads."

"And what about *you*, Rose?" he'd asked. "You talk about Steven and Anita and Susan, but what about Rose? How much do you need me…or want me?" he added softly.

"Well, of course…" she began, but he held up his hand and smiled sadly.

"If you can't say the right thing, then say nothing." He turned and left the apartment.

Joe, I think Charlie and I have problems, but I'm not sure how to fix them. I do know that if he spends more time out of the house than in, we'll be in real trouble.

She looked at the last paragraph and sighed. There lay the crux of the matter. She and Charlie were leading two separate lives. She'd been correct about one thing: writing it out had helped her to see.

She put her pen to paper again and signed off as usual…. *Yours forever, Rose.* She stopped. And read. *Forever.* She shivered, goose bumps covering her skin. It was hard to breathe. How could she give up Joe?

No wonder Charlie avoided her when the Dream Box was on her desk.

She added a postscript: *I know how to fix the problems between Charlie and me, but the price is too high.*

"It's quiet with the kids away at camp," Rose said on a Saturday morning, a month after the bar mitzvah. "I've got the whole day ahead of me with almost nothing to do. It feels weird."

Charlie eyed her over his cup of coffee. "How about spending the day with me?"

"With you? Aren't you going to the shops?"

"Just one, then I have to see a few accounts that have worked out well. It never hurts to shake hands with the clients."

It almost sounded like fun, and she was curious. "What should I wear?" asked Rose.

Charlie placed his cup carefully on the table. "You mean you'll come?"

Suddenly shy, she glanced down at her plate. "Why not? Except at the bar mitzvah, I've never seen you 'work a room.' This is my chance to see you in action with your customers. Maybe I'll learn something."

"What you'll learn is that, when I'm on the road, I'm the same charming guy you know at home."

She glanced up at him, in time to see a big smile cross his handsome face.

"Come on, Rosie. Let's mix some business with pleasure."

Thirty minutes later, with boxes of doughnuts lining their backseat, they arrived at his Bayside location. The three car bays were full, his staff working.

"We're a man short today, but the work's getting done," said Charlie. "Jimmy called me earlier. Come on. I want to compliment him and drop off the doughnuts for the guys."

"Absolutely," said Rose, getting out of the car. "It takes more than a salary to have a happy employee."

Her comment was met with silence. "What? Don't you agree?" she asked.

"One hundred percent," Charlie replied. "You surprised me, that's all. With you, it's always been the money."

"When you worry about food and shelter, it's always about the money," she retorted, "but even then a thank-you would be nice. It was like when I was sewing for the factories. I knew I was good because they gave me more work, but hearing an 'attagirl' or 'great job' would have been nice, too."

He kissed her then. A big one, right on the mouth just outside the office door.

"Charlie!" she squealed. She patted her hot cheeks, fanned herself and tried to catch her breath.

"That's in appreciation of all you've done, with my compliments and thanks and as many 'attagirls' as you want. And, Rosie," he added, "there's lots more where that came from."

He watched her, caution and amusement warring on his face, but his eyes twinkled and he chuckled.

She simply shook her head, bewildered, then amazed herself by laughing with him. That Charlie—he always managed to lighten her mood.

But she wasn't laughing at their next stop, which was Fred's Flower Shop, a fairly new customer of Charlie's. This was just one of Fred's four locations.

"Don't forget the doughnuts," said Charlie. "For the ladies in the office."

The ladies swarmed over Charlie as soon as he walked in. And it wasn't because of the doughnuts.

"I was hoping you'd show up today," said the receptionist, leaving her seat to greet Charlie. She stroked his cheek, tilted her head back. "Looking good, my man. Looking good."

Rose stared at the young woman whose dark hair was styled in a beehive and whose tight skirt and blouse left nothing to the imagination. The woman glanced at Rose and raised an eyebrow.

"Jill, this is my wife, Rose," began Charlie.

Jill's eyebrow shot higher, if possible, and Rose felt herself being examined from head to foot.

"Good morning, Jill," she said, extending her hand, forcing the other woman to step away from Charlie or look foolish.

A well-manicured hand with red polish slipped into hers. "Wife, huh?" She shrugged.

What did that mean?

"And this is Linda, the person who pays the bills and who loves chocolate-glazed doughnuts," said Charlie, directing Rose's attention to another woman.

"Then I'm especially glad to meet you, Linda," said Rose. "We appreciate your careful work and timely payments. Thank you so much."

"Oh, we love Charlie," Linda replied. "Always give him priority time." She winked. "And the doughnuts aren't bad, either."

What had she fallen into here?

The office door behind them opened, and a portly man emerged. Rose recognized him as Fred, the man who owned the business.

"Charlie! Rose! How nice to see you again. That was some party you threw for your boy last month. Come on in."

But Charlie shook his head. "We don't want to hold you up, Fred—unless there's something on your mind?"

"Not a thing. My trucks are running on time. That's all I ask for...besides a fair price." He glanced toward the desk. "Ah...doughnuts. Don't mind if I do," he said and helped himself.

"Okay, then," said Charlie. "Stay well, Fred. Ladies, see you next time."

Rose couldn't wait to get outside and breathe fresh air. A couple of shameless hussies. "Have they no scruples?" she asked her husband.

Charlie laughed. "They're just playing. It doesn't mean a thing. A little flirting breaks up their day."

"They're probably single..."

"I don't know," said Charlie. "Never thought about it."

"Oh, come on. They were all over you."

"All I want from them is to put my phone calls through when I need to talk to Fred. I want my bills paid on time, and I want my messages delivered with accuracy. If doughnuts help, I'll bring them."

"And flirt a little…"

He shrugged. "Whatever it takes."

Did he mean that? Rose wondered at their next stop. No young, blowsy girls here, but a sophisticated blonde named Michelle. The owner's charming wife who addressed almost every remark to Charlie. After their brief chat, Michelle invited Rose and Charlie to join her for lunch.

"Your husband makes me laugh," said the woman, with a quick glance at Rose before resting her gaze on Charlie. Her blue eyes darkened with interest and speculation, and Rose realized that it was this woman who might pose a real danger. The girls from the flower shop were nonstarters in comparison.

"Lunch?" asked Charlie, glancing at his watch. His expression reflected disappointment. "I'm sorry, Michelle. Maybe next time. Unfortunately we're on a tight schedule today."

A slow, inviting smile emerged. "I'll hold you to it, Charles. Maybe a table at Vincent's…like last time?"

Charlie stared at the woman. "Vincent's is fine. Tell Ralph to expect my call. I'm sorry to have missed him today."

Michelle shrugged. "Duty first. His daughter,

you know. I'm minding the store, so to speak, or at least the phones. He's expanding again. Something about new routes or new trucks, I'm not quite sure."

The phone rang just then, cutting off further conversation. Rose walked toward the exit and Charlie followed.

Her thoughts swirled so fast, she couldn't separate them for analysis. Was Charlie's sales time spent fending off women or were these the exceptions? Had he brought her to these particular places knowing what would probably happen? Hmm... that was an idea that required consideration.

"Ready?" said Charlie, holding the car door open for her.

"I'm ready for lunch," replied Rose, her words slow and deliberate. She tilted her head back to look directly at him. "Maybe Vincent's?" she drawled. "At a table for...two, shall we say?"

His green eyes widened, and at first Charlie simply stared at her, then he started to chuckle softly at first until finally he couldn't control himself and he started laughing.

"You're smart, Rose...a hell of a lot smarter than I. She caught me last time. Blindsided me. Ralph never showed. How'd you figure it out?"

Maybe men were easily led by a pretty woman— it happened in the movies all the time. "It wasn't hard, Charlie. She's rich and she's bored. That's a lethal combination."

"It was one of the worst meals in my life,"

admitted Charlie with an exaggerated shudder. "She wanted to talk about anything but business. A total waste of time."

But Rose's day hadn't been wasted. Perhaps these particular women meant nothing to Charlie. Sooner or later, though, there might be another one. One who excited him, made his heart race. Maybe he'd meet her at the bank when he wore his blue suit. Maybe she would be an entrepreneur through the chamber of commerce. A woman who thought he made the stars shine for her alone. A woman who might think Charlie was her *bershert*.

A surge of jealousy ripped through her, and she clutched the roof of the car to keep from falling. She'd known he would find his true soul mate one day. Hadn't she warned him when he proposed?

"Rosie! What's wrong?" Charlie helped her into her seat and squatted next to her. He took her hands. "Are you ill? Do you want to go home?"

She took a deep breath. "Maybe you shouldn't visit your customers on Saturdays. You can't be sure the proprietors are available so you'd be wasting time."

"What are you talking about? Why?"

"I—I think it's better that way."

After a moment, he asked, "Are you afraid my head will be turned by a girl in a tight skirt?"

Goodness, he was taking her on. "You admit you got blindsided once…"

"But I don't make the same mistake twice." He

leaned closer and kissed her gently, sweetly. "I love you, Rose. Don't you know that?"

"Yes. Yes, I do." She caressed his cheek. "Oh, Charlie," she whispered, her mouth against his. "You're...you're the best." *I don't deserve him.* She kissed him hard then snaked both arms around his neck. Her heart raced liked a runaway train, and she pulled him even closer. That was when he lost his balance and fell on top of her.

Immediately, wolf whistles vibrated through the air. Charlie managed to turn his head. Rose peered over his shoulder. Pedestrians were giving them a thumbs-up. Rose hid her face, but Charlie laughed until a tear escaped from the corner of his eye.

"I'd like to make one more visit," Charlie said a few minutes later, when he got behind the wheel, "and then we have the rest of the day free to do whatever we want."

"Sure," said Rose. "Which account?"

"Linder's Lumberyard."

Rose nodded, then bit her lip. Linder's was a solid company that had grown little by little since its beginning ten years before. Then, three years ago, Frank Linder had died unexpectedly of a heart attack.

"How's Mrs. Linder doing?" asked Rose.

Charlie shrugged. "Hanging on. Paying her bills." Concern laced his voice, but Rose knew it was for the woman, not for the bills.

Fifteen minutes later, they parked in the lot of the lumberyard and headed for the corner office inside the building. The smell of sawdust tickled their noses; the sound of electric saws cutting through boards pierced their ears.

A young boy—maybe nine or ten—was alone at the desk, flipping baseball cards, a wrinkle on his brow. As soon as he spotted Charlie, however, he jumped from his seat.

"Hi, Charlie!"

"Pete. How are you?" Charlie pumped the boy's arm.

"Mom's out there," he said, pointing to the busy working floor of the yard. "And so is Michael. Did you bring doughnuts? I'm hungry. Breakfast was a long time ago."

"Have two," said Rose, offering the box. "I'm Rose, Charlie's wife."

"Hi," he said while digging for a treat. He took one bite, then put the cake on the desk. "You know what?" he asked, his voice suddenly quivering. "Maybe I'm not too hungry."

"Not hungry?" asked Charlie, before leaning toward the boy and placing a hand on his shoulder. "What's wrong, son?"

Pete shrugged and brushed a lock of dark hair from his forehead. "It's Mom. She's…she's crying again all the time."

Rose's heart ached for the child. Whatever was happening in his family was confusing him. She glanced at Charlie. "She's been paying her bills, so the business is okay. It must be something else."

"Right," confirmed Charlie, looking through the window. "I see Marilyn coming now."

"Don't tell her what I said, Charlie. Okay?" asked Pete.

"It's our secret," said Charlie, winking at the boy.

Pete ran to the door when his mother opened it. "Mom! Charlie and Mrs. Charlie brought doughnuts."

Marilyn Linder wore no makeup, had pulled her brown hair back into a ponytail and in her work shirt and dungarees, she could have passed for a teenager—from the distance. Up close, Rose could see the toll stress had taken from the lines around her eyes to her pinched mouth and her thin frame.

But the woman's eyes lit up when she saw Charlie. Rose sighed. She was starting to get used to this pattern.

"Hello, Charlie. You must be Rose. Charlie talks about you all the time."

"I'm happy to meet you, Mrs. Linder. Pete's been entertaining us. He's a terrific boy."

Love shone on her face when Marilyn glanced at her son and tousled his hair. "Hi, baby. Hungry for lunch?"

The kid glanced at the doughnuts.

"That's dessert. Run to the fridge and get the sandwiches. Go find your brother, too."

When Pete left, Charlie simply said, "How are you, Marilyn?"

With those words, the tears came, but the woman held her head up and let them fall.

"I've decided to sell the business," she said. "I can't do this anymore."

Rose gave a soft gasp. Charlie would never, ever give up any of his locations. "That's a big decision," she said quietly.

The woman nodded. "Not easily made." She glanced at Charlie and waved her arm at the lumberyard. "This was Frank's dream," she said. "You know that."

"Frank started as a carpenter," she explained to Rose. "He built our house. He always dreamed of owning his own lumberyard. And he did it. He made it happen, and I've kept it going. But…" She twirled away from them as though suddenly needing her privacy. "But…it's not my dream."

Her voice was so soft, Rose could hardly hear her.

"Am I giving up my sons' inheritance if I sell? That question haunts me at night. What would Frank want me to do? What would he want?" Her voice quivered, full of agony, pain and doubt.

Rose winced.

"Sell it." Charlie's tone held no doubt at all. Rose stared at him, confused, and Marilyn turned so quickly, her ponytail whipped her cheek.

"You think so, too?" The woman looked at Charlie as though he were her savior.

"Yes, Marilyn, I absolutely do. For two reasons," said Charlie. "First, Linder's Lumberyard is making money, so you'll get a good price. At least a fair price."

The woman nodded. "I thought the same thing."

"Second," Charlie said more slowly, "I'm speaking as a friend now, Marilyn. Look at you. You're skin and bone. Would Frank want you to wear yourself out like this? The answer to that is no. He'd never want you to give up your life."

Rose understood his message now. "Your boys," she said, "need a healthy mother more than anything else. A strong mother. What good is a business if they lose two parents?"

"My brothers think I'm crazy," said Marilyn, tears falling again. "But look at me! I'm really a high-school English teacher, and I loved my job. What am I doing running a lumberyard?"

An English teacher? "Like my first husband," whispered Rose.

Marilyn stared at her. "You were married before Charlie?"

Rose nodded. "Joe died in the war."

"I'm sorry," Marilyn said. "I didn't know..."

"That's all right," Rose said quickly.

But Marilyn seemed to drift away for a moment, and when she spoke again, she sounded thoughtful, her words coming out with a big sigh. "Frank was my everything—my best friend, my partner. I've been alone for three years now. I think marrying someone else would be half a life. No—" she shook her head "—it's not for me."

Rose squeezed her hand. "Don't be too sure.

Charlie and I have two beautiful children together. And, of course, Susan. We're happy. Life's not so bad."

Then she glanced at her husband and saw the compassion that filled his eyes as he looked at Marilyn. Compassion and affection for the woman. Suddenly the hussies and harlots from the morning seemed more appealing to her.

·

That night, after making love with Rose, Charlie lay in bed watching her sleep. She may have been rattled that morning, but her thoughtful silence after leaving the lumberyard made him think Marilyn had shaken her up more than the other women simply by being her natural honest self. Or else Rose was pining for Joe again. He didn't think so this time.

His wife had no idea about all the opportunities he'd had to cheat on her since he'd started the business. Had he thought about it? Sure.

Had he done it? No.

Would he ever?

He couldn't swear to never, but he hoped not. He'd told himself over and over that if he couldn't have his wife's whole heart, working hard to build a successful business would be enough satisfaction for him.

He certainly hadn't gone into marriage with the intention of being a philanderer. And it hadn't been his goal to make her think he might be when they'd called on his customers that day. He'd just wanted to spend time with her. They'd never have a better opportunity to be alone than now when the kids were away. In his opinion, the day had gone very well.

After visiting the lumberyard, they'd meandered into Great Neck and stopped at CAR's third location. Rose was a hit there. She'd jumped right in and greeted customers, helped find prices of tires, researched any auto part they needed. Then he and Rose had driven around town sightseeing, looking at lovely homes. "One day we'll buy one," he'd said.

Of course, Rose didn't want to hear it. He'd planted the seed, however, and was happy with that. Funny how he always wanted to jump ahead, and she always wanted to hold back.

They'd gone to the movies and saw *The Miracle Worker,* then went out for a late dinner. At home again, they'd made love, and that, too, was a leisurely experience—until it couldn't be. Charlie grinned thinking about how in tune they were with each other, at least in that department.

Which had to mean she loved him, didn't it? She didn't "grin and bear" his touch. She enjoyed it. Or was she faking? Faking for fifteen years?

Damn it! He was driving himself crazy—again. Hadn't Rose said that very morning that "life wasn't too bad"? And now he was spoiling an almost perfect day in his almost perfect life.

PART THREE

Long Island

Chapter 11

The phone rang on Rose's desk. She reached for the receiver, her mind still on the quarterly estimated-tax filing she was preparing. She was happy with her work at this accounting firm—hadn't changed jobs since graduating. Two and two always equaled four, there were no maybes, no loose ends. She understood the tax laws and how to apply them. More importantly, the clients trusted her advice. She belonged in this world. "Teachman and Raskins. How can I help you?"

"Mama? Mama?"

She stopped thinking. Stopped writing. Never before had Susan called her *Mama,* at least not since she was two years old.

"What's wrong?" asked Rose.

"You don't know? Turn on the radio. The president's been shot."

"What president? Of your college?"

"No! No. President Kennedy. In Dallas. They've canceled classes here. My stomach's jumping…I'm going to be sick…"

Rose heard her retching and waited, helpless, wishing she had a radio at her desk.

When Susan returned to the line, Rose quietly said, "Sweetheart, listen to me. You are twenty years old now. An adult. You must keep your wits about you." Then she quickly added, "Where's Paul?" Her daughter shouldn't be alone when her heart was breaking.

"I—I don't know. I was in class. He probably was, too."

"Well, find him. Stay together."

"Everyone's crying, Mom. Even the boys. They're blaming the Russians. I want to come home."

"Then come," Rose replied immediately. "Come home."

The New York Times

New York, Saturday, November 23, 1963

KENNEDY IS KILLED BY SNIPER AS HE RIDES IN CAR IN DALLAS; JOHNSON SWORN IN ON PLANE

December 1, 1963

Dear Joe,

Susan and Paul arrived here together. The boy wouldn't leave her side. November 22 was a Friday, and the kids stayed with us for the weekend while the nation reeled with shock. Susan could barely talk. None of us had much to say; the catastrophe was difficult to absorb. We watched television round the clock. The whole country did. Americans are still grieving, and the world joins us.

Susan took your picture from her bedroom and held on to it day and night. At some point, she leaned against me and said, "I feel like I've lost him again. And yet, it's for the first time because I never met him."

I cried. Charlie hugged her. Twenty years later, she feels what it's like to lose a daddy and a hero.

Thank God for Charlie. He keeps his head. He knew exactly what to say. Except once when he had to stop and wipe his eyes.

We were all sitting in the living room when your daughter stated in a tone so flat that it scared me, "Evil has won. Camelot's gone... and all our dreams with it." As I stared at her, I saw myself reading the telegram that told me you were gone.

The silence following Susan's pronouncement hurt my ears. I couldn't find the right words to console her.

But Charlie knew what to say. "You're wrong, Susie Q. Evil will only triumph if good people do nothing. That's why Joe and I fought in the war. It's why people help one another.

It's why teachers teach and doctors cure. We all have our contributions to make, and we can only do that when we follow our dreams."

Your daughter heard him; Charlie had reached her. By the time she and Paul returned to school, I saw her natural spirit begin to reappear and was less worried.

She took your picture with her this time, but before she left I looked at it—at you—for a long while. You'll always be a hero in this family, Joe. A forever-young hero. Overflowing with dreams that cannot be realized, except perhaps for one—our child. Our Susan.

May you rest in peace and provide your daughter with hope. Amen.

Rose

P.S. Thank you for sending Charlie my way. I still wonder sometimes how personal that "pact" became. My loquacious husband keeps silent on this subject.

Rose slowly folded the front page of the *New York Times,* wrapped it in plastic and placed it and her letter in the manila envelope she kept next to the Dream Box on the closet shelf.

She rubbed her hands together, her nerves jangling from her temple to her toes, uneasy with the world changing again, a world she couldn't control. *The home front. Focus on the home front.* That was something she could do. She'd had years of experience creating a safe haven for her loved ones.

At that moment, however, after the week's turmoil, she needed one of her own.

She walked quickly to the living room and, like a heat-seeking missile, looked for Charlie. He was on the couch with Steven and Anita, the television still on, the volume low as the newscasters continued their broadcasts.

"We've had a terrible time, and we're in for more," Rose said.

He nodded. Waited.

She opened her arms. "But I want to dance with you, Charlie. Now. Come sing to me."

He stood immediately and went to her. Holding her, leading her in the dance while she listened to him sing Johnny Mathis.

"This is so nice, Charlie," she murmured, her head resting on his broad shoulder.

"'It's wonderful, wonderful,'" he sang.

She giggled.

Anita clapped. Steven wrinkled his nose and said, "Yuck."

The glimpse of normalcy sustained her. Relief made her weak. She wanted no more tragedies. No more surprises.

"But six months ago, Dad said that we have to fight for what we believe in, and I'm going!" Susan stood straight, her eyes blazing with purpose.

Rose couldn't breathe. Her baby wanted to go down south with a bunch of college students to register voters? She couldn't understand it. They'd be targets for sure. What happened to a peaceful life? To no more surprises?

"Everyone's entitled to one vote in this country, and the majority of Negroes aren't even registered in their home counties," continued Susan. "Don't worry, Mom. I'll be with a group. We're organized."

"And the Klan? They're not organized?" This was a nightmare. Her daughter was staging another nightmare. Rose silently appealed to Charlie. *Say something. Do something.*

"I'll go with them, Rose," he responded, his eyes alight, "for a week. You'll feel better about it just as you did when I went to Washington with her last year."

Her mouth opened and closed like a fish's. That was not the response she wanted. She put her hands to her head, slapped her ears. "Am I hearing correctly? You'll go with her?" Was it them, or was it she who was crazy?

"Why not? The business can run for a week without me."

"Charlie, are you out of your mind? What are you thinking? This isn't a peaceful march with Dr. King."

"I'm thinking it's the right thing to do. If Joe were here, he'd think so, too. He'd go."

She stepped toward him and jabbed him in the chest. "I'll tell you something about Joe. And about you. You're both nuts. I married two idiots, that's what I did. What kind of brain do I have?"

Charlie just laughed, picked her up and twirled her around as if she were a doll. "It's not your brain, Rosie. It's your heart. You have heart."

"Then don't break it, Charlie." She looked at Susan. "Or you."

"It's just for the summer, Mom. I'll be fine."

"Sure," whispered Rose. "I can see the headline now—Civil rights workers are *fine* in Mississippi." Incipient tears gathered and fell. "Excuse me. I have to lie down."

Her head throbbed. She swallowed an aspirin and sought her cool pillow. It was 1964, and Susan was twenty-one years old. Charlie and Rose had attended her college graduation last month. Summa cum laude and Phi Beta Kappa, Susan was one of the best and brightest from a group that was top-notch. But that didn't matter at all.

Her firstborn would fly away now, and Rose would have to accept it. She simply hadn't expected the initial flight to be so far. Or so dangerous.

August 4, 1964

Dear Joe,

She's alive. Some of the others aren't. Today, the bodies of three youngsters were found in an earthen dam in Mississippi. Susan knew the boys. She's devastated. And outraged. Scared, too. Newspaper headlines are blazing the story across the country; everyone's talking. The KKK murdered these kids after they were released from jail—arrested on speeding charges, I might add. A lot of bull!

I believe Susan's outrage will trump her fear. She's on a crusade to change the world. She believes she will practice tikkun olum *and repair the world.*

Don't ask about Charlie. The guilt he feels about leaving her in the Deep South after his one week there is killing him.

I offered platitudes of comfort: All's well that ends well. Don't look back. He waved me away with a "Please, Rose."

Then I blasted him. "Look in the mirror! What do you expect when she has you as an example?"

He had no idea what I was talking about. Since his work resettling displaced persons after the war, he's continued to help on a local level however he can. Sometimes with job training, always with fund-raising, and that's what the children see and hear around the house. He has a wonderful heart and he's made an impression on all of them, but especially on Susan.

Love, Rose

Long Island, 2007

The table in her mother's kitchen was now covered with a myriad of items from the Dream Box. Susan fingered Steven's bar mitzvah invitation.

"Paul and I felt so grown-up dancing together at the party. We were a couple, even then, and I looked pretty that night. The dress…" She closed her eyes picturing her younger self, then opened them again and glanced at Rose. "You really know clothes, Mom. You've got the eye." She shrugged. "I didn't inherit it."

"No," Rose said. "You've got more of Joe's traits."

With her mom's brief comment, Susan's stomach tightened. Her mother didn't often talk about Joe, and when she did, it was usually only as a passing reference. Even at sixty-three, Susan felt the excitement of a new revelation.

"You, Susan, study our world," began Rose. "The history, people, events, leadership by using facts. Your father studied it through literature—Shakespeare, Milton, Hardy, all the great plays, poetry and novels that reflect people's lives." She paused thoughtfully. "It seems to me that you both were after the same thing. You just went about getting there in different ways."

"All I ever wanted to do was fix the world," said Susan, beginning to laugh. "Some goal, huh? I guess it takes more than one lifetime."

"I'm thrilled you've had *this* lifetime," Rose said dryly.

Susan started, then understood. "Oh, Mom. Don't focus on my experiences that summer. Other things—good things—also happened then, like moving into this house. It's the coming year I'm worried about. The future. Matthew and Lizzy..."

"You must make your peace with Matt," said Rose. "And soon."

"I know, I know," she whispered, her hands fisting, her heart heavy. "He has to go off with a clear mind. I'll think of something. I'll talk to him. Maybe at the party tomorrow."

Susan studied the Dream Box again, more for the distraction of it than for renewed interest in the familiar objects. She picked up an envelope—the mortgage agreement with the bank. A mortgage that had been paid off years ago. "You used to throw the best parties right here in this house."

"That's the only reason we bought the place," said Charlie. "Great layout for parties. All your mother's idea."

Rose groaned. "Not quite...but I have no regrets." She peered over his shoulder at the mortgage papers. "I guess I never throw anything out," she sighed. "You're right about that summer, Susan. We bought this house in September 1964..."

Charlie hung up the phone, sat back in his comfortable chair in the Great Neck shop and began thinking of a sales pitch to use on Rose. Since he'd returned from Mississippi at the end of June, and especially since Susan had finally returned home, he and Rose had spent several Saturday afternoons driving. He'd always made sure to research a few homes for sale beforehand and managed to meander through those particular neighborhoods.

A Realtor had just called him about a certain property he and Rosie had seen on their forays, not that they'd gone inside. Oh, no. Exploring the interior was too much commitment for his wife. But there'd been an expression on her face when they'd passed this house. She'd even asked him to drive by again. Then she'd pressed her lips together.

Rosie and change…. Maybe all women were like that, but he didn't think so. His wife clung to what she had and built on it little by little. Risks? Hah!

But a home of their own. A backyard. Flowers, trees, space. The American dream. And why not? Buying a house was an investment, not a risk, especially with Rose's salary coming in. Hmm…now that he thought about it, she had become more relaxed since she'd started her career. There was nothing like a paycheck to imbue confidence in his wife.

Maybe he wouldn't need a sales pitch at all. Maybe she was ready to make the move. And if not, well, Charlie had a hidden ace.

He picked up the phone again. "Rosie? Let's go for a ride."

Two hours later, after delivering some doughnuts

to a customer on the way, Charlie pulled up in front of 46 Maplewood Lane. The ranch-style brick house had a charming front porch and stood on a wide lot, second from the corner on a quiet, shady street. A grassy lawn and well-tended greenery presented a pretty picture. The entire setup was as different from where they lived now as could be. Suddenly, the quiet made *him* pause. Then he laughed at himself. The city boy could adjust to the suburbs.

"Ah," said Rose. "The For Sale sign's still here. Now I understand." But she didn't get out of the car. "Have you been inside yet?"

"No."

"I hope I hate it."

"No, you don't."

"Charlie, money will be tight. Very tight. The business is still paying off bank loans from the expansion, and a house requires a mortgage. Even with what I earn now...we'll be poor again. No," she said. "Let's wait a couple of years. There's no rush."

"Prices only go up, Rosie. You know that. You give your clients financial advice all the time. A house is an investment as well as being a home for the family."

"We already have a home. As for clients, well, it's easier to give advice than to take it. Oh," she moaned, "I'm getting a stomachache."

He'd anticipated every one of her objections and was ready to counter. "The timing is perfect, Rose. Steven is starting high school and Anita, junior high school. They'd start fresh in new schools with other new kids from the various local elementary schools."

She tapped her fingers on her purse. "I'm roasting in the car." She opened her door.

Charlie glanced at his watch. The Realtor hadn't arrived yet. "Let's just walk…"

But Rose was already at the corner, looking down the cross street, then down Maplewood. Then she scanned the backyards, focusing on the one at Number 46. She tapped her lip. Shook her head. She walked toward him.

Now what? Charlie wondered.

"We'd be house poor," said Rose. "For starters, the windows are large and require drapes. I'd be sewing until I was blind."

"Who said you'd have to sew?"

"Men! Do you know the cost of material and labor? Think of your auto parts…it's the same thing. It's less expensive to do it yourself."

A car pulled up to the house and parked. The seller's Realtor.

"Rose," said Charlie, ready to play his ace, suddenly afraid she'd stalk away and not even enter the house. "Marty called me this morning at the shop."

Her eyes narrowed. "Don't tell me. Not again. Darn that Edith! She and Marty have been looking at houses forever, so why didn't she call me if they actually bought one?"

"It's not official yet, but they've made an offer. Five minutes away from here, Rosie. Our kids would be in the same school district with Anna." He didn't have to remind her that Aaron and Maddy were already living in Long Island with their two daughters, about ten miles farther east. They'd stayed in Brooklyn only a couple of years before trekking to the Island.

"Marty doesn't have other business loans to pay," she said.

The Realtor came over, shook their hands and said, "I've got the key if you're ready to go inside."

The problem, thought Rose, was that she was more than ready. She already loved the house from the moment she'd seen the welcoming front porch. And when she'd spotted the maple and birch trees in the backyard, providing blessed shade on a hot summer's day, she knew she was in trouble. They weren't ready for this. She tried to focus on the negatives. Besides, Charlie had manipulated her again, but at least he hadn't taken action without her.

She reached for his hand and squeezed it. "Okay. Let's go inside."

Thirty minutes later, Rose was in major trouble. The house was everything she could have wanted. In addition to the front porch, there was a flagstone patio in back for outdoor parties. She pictured family gatherings and cookouts on the grill.

The master bedroom had its own little suite with a private bath and a nook for reading…and a closet big enough to qualify as a small bedroom! The main rooms flowed one into the other, perfect for entertaining.

A fairy tale.

"The asking price on this is what?" She faced the Realtor.

He replied.

"I'm a plain woman," said Rose, "and I'll be plainspoken. It's too high. Much too high. Even... fifteen percent less is too high. Maybe the owners aren't serious about selling."

The man almost choked. Charlie almost did, too, and she hoped he'd keep his mouth shut.

"But to show that *we* are serious buyers," she continued, "we'll make a serious offer—of course, depending on engineering inspections and so forth. Would you prefer we do it through another agent? I think Charlie simply called you." She nodded toward the sign on the lawn.

"That would be fine. Actually better."

They exchanged information.

Three days later, Rose and Charlie went to contract at a fair price, according to Rose: ten percent less than asking. "I bought leeway to cover the windows," she explained to Charlie that evening as they got ready for bed.

"You're really something, Rosie."

"Me? Pish-tush. Fair is fair. The seller was testing the market, but our offer was adequate. I'll tell you what I am, Charlie Shapiro," she said while unbuttoning her blouse. "I'm your partner in this life we have. Your *equal* partner. Believe me, if I weren't bringing in a good salary plus bonus now, we'd stay right where we are, in our co-op, and be happy doing it." She poked him in the chest. "In fact, I'm still content here. So I'm glad you're a proud home owner, but you didn't pull this purchase off by flying solo."

With impatient movements, she got rid of her blouse and tossed it on a chair. Her skirt quickly followed. Then she shook her head and hung the items in the closet, all the while feeling Charlie's eyes on her.

"Not once, since I met you, have I wanted to fly solo."

His quiet words reverberated with meaning and with truth. She understood both, and her eyes stung at the compliment. He walked to her, reached for her, and his kiss was tender, a promise as though they were in their beginning years together.

The mood didn't last—it couldn't—not when the spark of contact ignited into a familiar flame. She saw his eyes darken, felt her own breath shorten, as his fingers traveled through her hair. His tender kisses turned into the impatient moves of a teenager, but it didn't matter.

As one, they fell across the bed. Her bra disappeared, then her slip. She looked up into the loving eyes of the man she'd married eighteen years before and felt a strange serenity take hold—even in the midst of their lovemaking, which wasn't serene at all.

It was a lot of fun.

Like kittens tumbling over one another, they rolled on the bed intertwined, first her on top, then him, until they caught their rhythm and quickly turned into tigers locked together face-to-face. How his fingers managed to find every one of her pleasure points, she didn't know. And as he touched and stroked her, she couldn't think at all. Her breasts swelled. He feathered her nipples and she squirmed, then screamed almost soundlessly. Oh, God. Colors drenched her mind. Yellow changed to orange, which turned to red. Red hot. So hot. She couldn't take more, not one more second…she reached for Charlie…

"Thought you'd never…" he gasped.

And then…they disappeared together until total collapse. She couldn't move, couldn't talk. But talking had never been Charlie's problem.

"You sure know how to kill a guy, Rosie—thank God. But if a robber broke in now, I'd just have to lie here and watch him."

She giggled. "I'm not worried," she replied as her breathing returned to normal. "You'd manage to hit him with…with…" She looked around the room and came up blank. She gazed down at him. "Hmm…well, that bat's no good anymore…"

He growled and pulled her to his side, covering her face with kisses. "You little devil, but I love you, sweetheart."

She nestled close. "Sleep tight, dear." She yawned and started drifting off, then heard Charlie sigh.

"What's wrong?" she mumbled in her sleep.

"Nothing," he whispered.

A kiss landed gently on her cheek.

Chapter 12

"**P**lease, please, pretty please, Daddy! You know they're great and they're coming to New York. Isn't Paul McCartney just so cute? He's my favorite. And all my friends are going…and… I'll never ask you for anything else again as long as I live!"

Anita's ponytail bounced with every step, jump and motion of her body. Wiry and full of energy like her mother but with an unquenchable confidence, Charlie's daughter was a challenge. It would be very easy to say yes to anything she wanted. The twelve-year-old was simply adorable.

But adorable or not, Charlie learned early on to take the coward's way. "What does Mommy say?"

"Uh…she knows about it." Anita peeked up at him.

Here we go again. "The whole country knows about the concert. What did your mother say?"

A long, heavy sigh emanated from deep inside

his daughter. "Nothing. I didn't ask yet. I think you should just tell her I can go. I know she won't let me. She'll be afraid."

"Anita sweetheart, *I'm* afraid. There will be thousands of people at Shea Stadium, and you're one little girl."

"But Aunt Gertie is working the concert. I'll be near her."

Not quite. "We've gone to see the Mets play ball. Be reasonable, Anita. The ballpark is huge, and your aunt will be busy. She can't watch you."

Her mouth started working, her complexion turned red. The tears would start at any moment. He hated that.

"You—" gasp "—took Steven all the way—" gasp "—to California for a stupid baseball game in a big stadium just like Shea. This concert is right here in New York. It won't cost so much."

He needed to buy time. "How are your grades?"

"Good." She brightened.

Of course Anita's definition of *good* and Susan's definition were miles apart, but each child brought her own magic to the family. As he looked at his daughter, hope lit her hazel eyes, and Charlie knew he'd think of something to convince Rose it was all right.

"We'll give it a go," he said. "But in the meantime…" He extended his arm and sang "I Want to Hold Your Hand."

"Oh, Daddy!" Anita shook her head and giggled, then joined him for the verse. Harmonizing, they walked into the house on Maplewood Lane.

Hearing their blended voices made Rose want to sing, too. Wisely, she didn't. Charlie finally had someone to sing duets with him. But the song? Performed by four skinny boys with mops of hair. She shrugged. What did she know? Charlie thought they had a sound, something different. Not like the Beach Boys, and certainly not like the Peter, Paul and Mary folk-song crowd.

Rose understood only two things: Anita couldn't stop drooling over Paul McCartney, and Steven thought he was the next Ringo Starr. Rose and Charlie had bought him a set of drums and the noise never stopped. Thank goodness the house had a full basement with a door at the top of the stairs.

They'd been in Great Neck for almost a year now, and Rose had no regrets. They hadn't spent one cent on furnishings, but she had made progress with the window treatments, and the house was starting to feel like home. The kids had adjusted to their new schools, Edith and Marty were five minutes away, Aaron and Maddy twenty minutes east, and Charlie? Well, Charlie walked the property every night after work before he came into the house like a proud landowner of olden times. She teased him often, calling him "the king of all he surveyed."

"It wouldn't mean much without the queen," he replied, but she saw the pleasure in his eyes as he examined the shrubbery, even when he mowed the lawn.

"Time to wash up for dinner," she told the two singers when they joined her in the kitchen. "And don't go near the oven," she added, grabbing two pot holders and reaching inside to clasp the roasting pan filled with chicken.

They all heard Anita's stomach rumble.

"The sooner you set the table, the sooner we'll eat," said Rose, placing the pan safely on the stove top.

Anita glanced at her father. "Ask her, Dad."

"Ask me what?"

"About the Beatles concert," began Charlie.

Rose tilted her head. "You want to go?"

"Him?" Anita asked, wide-eyed, incredulous. "It's me, Mom! I want to go. It's mostly for kids."

"Really?" asked Rose. "Only kids? Does that mean I have to return our tickets?"

It took a moment for her message to sink in. But in that time, she grabbed her camera and started snapping pictures of two people whose mouths hung open.

"Finally," Rose gasped between her peals of laughter, "I finally got you. And got you good. Just look at your faces!" She climbed onto a chair, opened the cabinet door over the fridge and pulled out a fat envelope. She handed it to Charlie and watched.

"One, two…five, six tickets." He glanced at her questioningly.

"I couldn't leave out Paul—Susan would kill me." She turned to Anita and froze. Her daughter was crying. Sobbing.

"What, Anita? What's wrong?"

"I'm so…so happy! I never really thought… You know what?"

"No…" Rose replied slowly as she made her way down until she stood on the floor again. "What?"

"When I grow up, I'm going to be a singer. I'm going to write good songs, better 'n what I write now. And I'm going to give concerts, and you can have all my money. Then you won't have to sew curtains anymore."

Rose crushed her daughter to her in a hug and kissed her. "Thank you, *mamele,* but you can keep your money. Mommy's already very, very rich."

Saturday, September 25, 1965

Dear Joe,

Just wanted to let you know that Susan started graduate school this month. She's still at Columbia where she's living in the graduate dorm. She's in a special program that will lead to a Ph.D. without needing the master's. She's very happy about the whole thing. I'm happy about her job. The History Department hired her as a graduate assistant, which means she teaches introductory classes and leads small group discussions.

Paul is still in her life, very much so. He's following the same track in economics as she is in history. No talk about marriage yet, which is just as well, I suppose, seeing they're both focused on their careers and earn a pittance for their work.

Rose paused a minute and glanced at her watch. Charlie would be home soon; she'd better hurry and finish this, but she just had to tell him about the concert...

Last month, we were among fifty-five thousand people who crammed into a ballpark to watch four boys from England called the Beatles make music. There was so much screaming, however, that we could barely hear the songs. For another $1.25 I bought one program as a souvenir. Who knows? It might be valuable some day. Charlie says these guys are good. I trust his opinions about music, but I prefer Frank Sinatra myself.

Actually, she trusted Charlie's opinions more and more these days. Sometimes she agreed with him, and she always laughed now each time he said, "Rosie, I drag you kicking and screaming whenever we do something new. In the end you're always happy we did it. Stick with me, baby, and you'll be all right."

Of course, without her, it was Charlie who'd be in trouble. He jumped before looking. Spent without saving. He was a risk taker. She'd insisted they cut all extra spending since moving into the house. The concert had been the family's Hanukkah present—early Hanukkah present—for this year. No one had complained.

> *So long for now, Joe. I'll write again on Susan's birthday unless something else important comes up.*
> *Love, Rose*
> P.S. *Your daughter never returned your picture to me, and I never ask for it. You belong more to her now although a corner of my heart tears whenever I think of you.*

Later that same Saturday afternoon, Charlie ambled through the front door, the day's mail in his hand. Rose sat at the kitchen table reading a hefty novel. He recognized *Gone with the Wind* not only for its size, but because she'd complained about it keeping her up until 2:00 a.m.

"The responses are starting to come in quickly," he announced, staring at an envelope from Oklahoma.

She kept reading.

"More vets are showing up for the reunion than we thought."

Nothing.

"The house is on fire."

Seemed like an average husband couldn't compete

with Rhett Butler. Charlie unfolded one of the letters he held. Tommy Green, the Okie, was coming to the reunion with his wife. So was Henry Johnson from Iowa. Good.

Hank had written:

I'm glad we didn't wait the whole twenty-five years to get together. We lost Bill Livesay to a heart attack last November. Who knows how many more we'll lose to natural causes before the party? Thanks for suggesting the change of date and organizing this. See you in March. I'm looking forward to meeting Rose.

Hank, who can still make a good corn bread.

Charlie had no doubt. The man had gotten chummy with the army cooks and, when time allowed, would whip up something out of nothing. His buddies would scoff it down.

"Rosie," he said, "buy Susan a new dress. We're taking her with us. Why don't you buy yourself a new dress, too. There are a lot of guys who want to meet you."

He'd gotten her attention then.

"They'll be disappointed," she said. "I'm just an ordinary woman."

Charlie knew better and swallowed a pang. "No, Rose. You're special. They'll think of you as Joe's wife. Joe talked about you, told stories about you, and we ate them up. You'll still be Joe's wife—even after twenty years."

* * *

The Tavern on the Green at Sixty-seventh and Central Park West provided a private dining room—the Elm Room, which actually wrapped around an elm tree—for the reunion. Sparkling chandeliers hung from the ceiling, and every table had a pristine white cloth with a floral bouquet in the center. The Victorian structure itself could have distracted Rose if she hadn't been more intent on the men and women who arrived for the event.

Charlie had made the arrangements with the restaurant and acted as host. As his army buddies arrived, Rose stood next to him, smiling, shaking hands and surreptitiously rubbing her own on her skirt to get rid of the recurring dampness. No question about it, her nerves were jumpy because Charlie had been right. Each man identified her as Joe's wife.

"Hello, Rose. I feel I know you because of Joe. Charlie, you're a lucky son of a gun," said one veteran.

"Joe was a great guy. We called him the rabbi, did you know that? I'm happy to meet you, Rose," said a second.

"Funny how things work out," said another vet, looking at Charlie. "I guess you didn't waste any time visiting her when you got home, eh, Charlie?"

Rose glanced sharply at the man, glanced at her husband's pale face and said, "He could barely walk when he got home. He didn't visit for a while. But, eventually, life has to go on."

"Yes, ma'am."

The others saluted Charlie, nodding their approval.

"For marrying the prettiest woman in the room," he murmured to her.

"No," she said. "For not allowing 'Joe's wife' to remain alone." Surprisingly, she was getting tired of that public identity. She hadn't been Joe's wife in… good Lord, it had been twenty-five years.

"You know that's not why I proposed," Charlie said, his mind obviously still on the last GI's remarks. "Any one of these galoots would have scoffed you up—for Joe's sake, as well as for their own. But I didn't."

She squeezed his arm. "I know, Charlie. I know. Let's go mingle now. Susan's already introduced herself to everyone." Rose watched with pride as the young woman, wearing a fashionable red A-line dress that Rose had made for her, engaged in conversation with people she'd never before met.

"Look at her, Rosie. She's Joe's daughter through and through," said Charlie. "Just watch how everybody gathers around her to talk and listen."

Her husband had no clue. "You must be kidding. She's *your* daughter, Charlie. You're the people magnet. Susan's watched you her entire life. She's as much your daughter as Joe's."

She saw his Adam's apple bob a couple of times before he could speak. "You really think so?"

"Absolutely." From the corner of her eye, Rose

noticed her daughter take out a pad and pencil and begin to write as she chatted.

"I wonder what she's doing."

In unison, they walked toward her.

As soon as Susan spotted them, she beamed. "Dad, you've got the best friends. Brave friends. I'm going to interview them about their experiences…"

A familiar faraway look appeared in Susan's eyes. Her daughter was chasing ideas.

"It could be my doctoral dissertation," she murmured, "but it might be hard on you, Mr. Johnson." She looked at Hank from Iowa. "I'll ask a lot of questions."

"I have stories," the man replied. Then he stared at Charlie. "When I got back to my farm in '45, you know who was there?"

Charlie didn't have a chance to reply. No one else offered a response.

"German POWS," the man said. "They were working my land. Hell, they were a bunch of farm boys in their country, and they were doing a great job, but do you think I liked it? They were healthy, well fed and even socialized in town. While they were here in the USA, we were going through hell as prisoners! Starving. There were worms in our gruel, and we ate them. Ate them for protein," he explained to Susan.

"We starved and we froze in those hellholes. I'd lost so much weight, I couldn't drive a plow when I got home." The man's pain was hard to watch.

"Maybe this wasn't such a good idea," Susan said.

"Oh, yes it is," replied Hank immediately. "It's just that…" He paused and gathered himself, then looked at Charlie again. "We don't talk about the war much. Do we?"

"No, Hank. We sure don't. We got busy living again." He wrapped his arm around his old buddy. "Come on. I'll buy you a drink." They walked toward a roaming waiter.

"He's a hero, Mom," said Susan. "Every one of them is. Those who returned and those who didn't."

"So write about them, Susie Q. Tell their story, a soldier's story. The story about the Bulge."

Susan scribbled something that Rose couldn't see. "How about this?" she asked and held out her pad. Soldier Heroes: GI Joe and the Battle of the Bulge.

"Perfect. Just perfect." Rose began to cry.

Two hours later, as the dinner plates were being cleared away, Charlie stood and tapped his glass to get the crowd's attention.

"It seems that I'm the emcee for this shindig," he began, "so I get to make the rules—at least for tonight."

Chuckles and groans filled the room.

"I have a couple of questions," said Charlie. "Show of hands, please—how many of you went to college on the GI Bill?"

No shyness about that question.

"I ate it up. Became a lawyer."

"Nothing was too hard."

"School was different."

Charlie said, "Or maybe it was us who were different. Even I got all A's, and Rosie didn't have to nag too much."

"My husband's a comedian," Rose piped up. Her complexion turned a beautiful pink, and Charlie thought she must have surprised herself. His body stirred.

"What about jobs?" he asked, trying to get back on track.

The businessmen outnumbered the farmers, and those living in suburbia outranked those in the cities. After those responses, Charlie offered the floor to anyone who wanted to say something.

"You can make any kind of speech you want, and no one will shut you up. How often does that happen?"

One man stood. "I've got to say something to the young lady with you, Charlie." He looked at Susan. "Honey, I want you to know about Joe. I remember when he found out your mom was pregnant with you. He was so happy. Promised us each a cigar when we got home…. And what a storyteller he was. I wouldn't have made it without Joe's stories…"

"And I wouldn't have made it without Charlie's songs," said another. "Remember him singing in the foxholes… Damnation, that was sweet!"

"Are you still singing, Charlie?"

"Only in the shower," Charlie replied through his choked-up throat. He'd forgotten about the cigars.

"Except for tonight." He motioned Susan toward him. "Would you read this list when I tell you?"

His glance swept the group. "On your feet, soldiers. Atten-hut!"

They complied immediately, and he said, "This is for our buddies who didn't make it home. We'll never forget you." He nodded at Susan.

Susan called out the name of one fallen soldier at a time, Joseph Abraham Rabinowitz among them. Tears rolled down her face, but she never stopped reciting the names. When she was finished with that sad roster, Charlie began to sing "Taps": "'Day is done; gone the sun…'"

No one moved. No air stirred, except for Charlie's strong tenor, which flowed beyond the dining room and into the corridors until the final words, "'All is well, safely rest. God is nigh.'"

When the last note faded, he heard the sobbing. From his pals. From his daughter. From strangers who stood in the doorway.

"Sir," a man addressed Charlie. "I was at Normandy Beach…second wave…"

"Come in. Come in. You're welcome here," said Charlie.

By the time dessert was served, he was wrung out and sat quietly while Rose wiped his forehead. He rejoiced in her touch, in her attention.

"Next time," he said, "we'll get a place with music and dancing."

"Sure," she murmured.

"Hey, that's a good idea," said Daniel Jones from Pennsylvania, who, with his wife, shared a table with Charlie and Rose. "We need to end the evening on a happy note. Besides, Millie and I don't often get to go out on the town like this."

Rose jumped to her feet, her eyes snapping. "Well, Daniel, the lack of music never stopped us from dancing before." She extended her hand to Charlie. "Come on." She opened her arms. "Sing to me."

Everyone's eyes were upon her. He was there in a heartbeat.

"Join us," he called. "'Hold me close and hold me fast…'" he began to sing.

Amazingly, other couples did stand up and dance near their tables—a tight fit to be sure—but dancing felt right. At least, right to Charlie. His life was a rose right now, in this moment. He planned to soak up this ephemeral moment as Rose showered all of her attention and care on him.

At the end of the evening, after reluctant good-byes and after more reunion plans were made for five years later, Rose and Charlie drove Susan to her dorm.

"I'm wiped out," she said, getting into the car, "but it was one of the best evenings of my life. If you don't mind, I'm going to take a short nap. Wake me when we get there."

"No problem," said Charlie. "Too bad Paul is sick."

"Yeah," she agreed. "He would have loved it."

When he glanced into the rearview mirror a few

minutes later, he couldn't see her. "Rosie, look behind you. Is she really sleeping?"

He heard her low laugh. "Sure is."

"That paper she's writing," he began. "The dissertation?"

"Yes?"

"It will be his eulogy, Rose. She doesn't realize it yet, but her project will be a eulogy for every man we lost." He took a breath. "And maybe afterward, after you read it…you won't have to keep reading his letters. Maybe," he said quietly, "you can find peace."

She grabbed his elbow, and the car fishtailed on the road. "Are you crazy?" he yelled, shattering the solemn mood. "What are you doing?"

"I'm fine, Charlie. I'm happy. I *am* at peace."

Was she? Maybe the life they had was all she was capable of, and he didn't have a right to complain. *He* was the needy one, still needing to hear the words she didn't say. He wouldn't ask for them, though. She had to give them freely. He was the one who needed to come to terms. Rose might never say the three words he wanted to hear.

The year after the reunion, in the fall of 1967, Charlie sat in Steven's bedroom. It was a mess. How could an empty room be a mess? He shook his head, not knowing whether to laugh or cry. His boy was a college man now—under duress—and Charlie simply didn't know if he and Rose had done the right thing.

According to Steven, if he couldn't play professional ball, he wanted to work with Charlie. He loved
the business. He loved cars. Why did he need college?

Charlie heard Rose's steps outside the doorway
and looked up. She stared at him, then at the
wrinkled sheets he sat on, then at the stuff that was
still strewn around.

"He's a hundred miles away. It's not the moon,"
she said, but she bit her lip, her voice full of bravado.

"College isn't the right choice for everyone,"
said Charlie.

"In this family, it is." Now she sounded like the
Rose he'd married. "I'm telling Anita the same
thing. The question is not *if* you go to college, but
where you go to college."

"I'm not sure…"

"All his friends are in school, Charlie. What
would he do at the end of the day after working with
you? Stay in his room alone?" Rose shook her head.
"No. He belongs in school." Her mouth tightened.

"You're afraid," said Charlie, "and you're trying
to convince yourself otherwise."

She was silent for such a long minute that Charlie
was starting to become afraid himself.

"I know I'm right—in theory," Rose replied.
"But I hated seeing him so unhappy." Her deep sigh
sounded like a moan. "Every child is different… I
know he's not Susan, and that's all right, but he left
here angry and disappointed this morning. That's
not my Stevie."

Charlie stood up. "Grab a sweater. We're taking a ride to Albany."

"Wha—?"

"We're bringing him home. You just said the words that made sense. 'That's not my Stevie.' You're right. He's never been so insistent, so upset. He doesn't have the words to explain himself so we can understand. Hell, what teenage boy does more than grunt?"

A sad chuckle emanated from her. "Charlie, being a parent is…hard. Very, very hard." She looked over her shoulder as she left the room. "I'm getting my sweater and a map of the campus. Let's go."

But Steven wasn't in his dorm when they showed up three hours later. Young people were everywhere; in fact, some parents were still on campus, looking as haggard as Charlie felt. The residence-hall assistant showed them his student list. Steven's name had not been checked off.

"Either he hasn't shown up yet, or he didn't check in with us."

"But…but he left the city this morning," said Rose.

"There are a lot of residence halls," said Charlie. "He could have made a mistake. Or been transferred." He looked at the young man who'd started toward the desk.

"Probably not, but I'll make some calls."

Rose paced; Charlie gazed at the front doors. After ten minutes, the dorm assistant returned.

"I'm really sorry, but he's not at any other residence hall. He might have met up with some friends and they're helping each other unload. It's possible he got lost."

"We've been here before. My son's sense of direction is excellent."

"Could he have had an accident?" Rose whispered. "Oh my God…he could be in a hospital."

He cupped Rose's cheek. "We would have received a phone call, sweetheart."

"But we haven't been home for a few hours… Call Anita. See if—"

The assistant waved to them. "Phone call."

Charlie grabbed the receiver. "Hello."

"Daddy, it's Anita. Steve called. He's not at school, but he gave me a number."

Charlie wrote it down.

"Did he say anything else, honey?"

"Y-yes." Her voice shook when she spoke. "He said he was enlisting…he's joining the army."

Charlie couldn't breathe. He glanced at Rose, who was standing next to him. Her nose looked pinched, her mouth trembled, she kept rubbing her hands on her thighs.

He showed the college boy the number. "Is this local?"

"Yeah."

Charlie dialed. The receptionist at Motel 21 answered, and he was connected to Steven's room. He heard his son answer.

"It's Dad, Steve. Talk to me." Rose gripped his arm.

"I'm not college material."

"Well, I don't agree, but we can discuss that, hopefully in person. Mom and I are at your dorm. Where's the motel?"

"What? You're at the university?" His shock reverberated through the wires.

"We were worried about you so we drove up."

Steven was silent for a moment. "Maybe you should come here where there's privacy. Mom's going to freak out."

And I'm not? His heart pounding, Charlie got the directions to the motel. If Steven had really done what Anita said, Rose would more than "freak out." Charlie couldn't break down, as well, but he had to prepare her somehow.

"Rosie," he said as they walked to the car. "I'm going to ask you to remember one of your favorite sayings when we talk with Steven."

"As long as he's all right, I'll be fine." She smiled at him, a tight little smile, but she was trying.

"Just remember to keep your wits about you," he said with emphasis. "No matter what Steven says, stay cool."

"You're scaring me again, Charlie. What did he do?"

"I don't know for sure," he replied, which was the truth, but allowed him to buy some time.

When they walked into Steven's motel room, though, the first thing they saw was a fat envelope with U.S. Armed Forces stamped in the corner.

"Steven! What have you done?" Rosie cried out.

"What have I done, Mom? Well, for one thing, I've gotten your attention."

Rose's eyes bulged, she started to sway, and Charlie stood next to her. "No fair, Stevie," Rose protested. "When have you not had my attention? Every one of you kids."

Charlie held her and felt her whole weight as she leaned against him. "Easy, Rosie. Easy. Let's everyone sit down before we fall down."

When Rose was resting against the pillows on the bed, Charlie reached for the envelope. "Want to tell me what this is all about?"

Steven jumped to his feet. "You didn't listen! Either of you. All last year and all summer, I've been telling you I don't want to go to college. At least not yet. But somehow, between you and Mom, I took the SATs, the applications were sent, the deposits were sent. I don't even know how it all happened. And here I am—where I don't want to be."

"You'd rather be in Vietnam?" asked Charlie. "You'd choose to fight in a steaming hellhole instead of being in school?"

"I'd rather be where I'm useful," Steven replied. "You won't let me work with you, so I might as well fix engines in the army. The recruiter said that with my background, I'd probably be assigned to a motor pool."

Charlie held up his hands. "Let's back up. Did you actually sign those papers? Is it a done deal yet?"

Steven's gaze met his. "No. Tomorrow."

He heard Rose's gasp and pressed her hand. She was a strong woman, but when it came to those she loved, especially the children...

"Charlie," she whispered. "We came up to take him home. Remember? Before we left the house, that's what we said."

"What?" Steven said in disbelief. "Now?"

"Steve, let's you and I take a little walk," said Charlie. He glanced at Rose. "See you later. Try to relax."

Her glare could have ignited wood, but she waved them off.

The motel parking lot wasn't scenic in the evening, but Charlie barely noticed. How should he start? What could he say that would make a difference, that wouldn't be insulting to his sensitive son? He waited until they'd walked the length of the lot before speaking.

"I'm proud of you, Steven. Not for this drama, but for the thought behind it. I like being useful, too."

"I'm eighteen, Dad. I can make my own decisions."

Charlie swallowed a groan. "You're a young man, Steve. On the way to being a man of experience, but you're not there yet." He spoke slowly, choosing every word carefully. "It takes time to gain perspective, to understand how the world works."

"Well you sure don't get world perspective in college. As far as I can tell, Susan will be in school forever. She'll never get a job."

Charlie would have laughed if the situation

weren't so serious. "We're talking about you, Steven, not your sister. I have some ideas for you to consider that you might find appealing. And that your mother can accept."

Steven put his hand on Charlie's shoulder. They both stopped walking. "You know what, Dad? I think being the man is the hardest job in the family."

Charlie caught him in a headlock. "Now I know you're a genius. Just keep the thought to yourself—your mom won't appreciate it."

Thirty minutes later, they returned to the room. Rose blinked sleepily at them for a second. Then she was on full alert. Charlie was amazed she'd dozed at all. She must have been totally wiped out.

"Talk to me," she said. "One of you talk to me."

Steven spoke. "I'll come home after one semester—since you already paid for it—and transfer to night school while I work for Dad during the day. He managed his life that way, and so can I. I'm also going to try to get a part-time job here. Volunteer some time at places that fix cars for disadvantaged folks for free."

"And the army?" asked Rose.

"We're taking it one semester at a time," said Charlie. "The army isn't going away. If he wants it, it will be there for him, but next time he'll go for all the right reasons. Not just to get his parents' attention."

Chapter 13

June 2, 1968, almost midnight

Dear Joe,

Your daughter will now be known as Dr. Susan R. Shapiro. We watched her march down the aisle at her graduation ceremony this afternoon, along with her fiancé, Paul Grossman—yes, they're getting married, finally!—and I cried my eyes out.

More news—Susan's dissertation will be published by a New York publishing house. She dedicated it to you and Charlie, her two dads. So, by next winter, Soldier Heroes: GI Joe and the Battle of the Bulge *will be available in bookstores.*

Her accomplishment is almost unbelievable. I know that she's put her heart and soul into this work—the research, interviews and,

*of course, the writing. I'm hoping she can
come up for air now and that she and Paul can
start a real life.*

Rose paused, shifting herself into a more comfortable position on the couch. She couldn't
sleep despite the very full day—or maybe because of
it. After the commencement, the Shapiro and Grossman families celebrated at Tavern on the Green. Conversation was nonstop. Paul had been getting offers
from Wall Street firms; Susan loved the university en-
vironment.

"So," Rose had said during all the career talk,
"when are we fitting in a wedding?"

"Hmm…we've already got an apartment rented,"
said Susan a little absentmindedly. "Anytime, I
suppose. We want something small, Mom. Just the
family." She looked at Paul. "What do you think?"

"I think your mom is going to keel over."

She certainly had felt like keeling over. College
degrees or not, they weren't living together like
hippies. She turned to Charlie. "Call over the
maître d'. We're planning a wedding—right now."

"Mom!" her daughter had gasped. "I'm not
pregnant or anything."

"And you won't be…until after you're married."

At that point, Steven had roared with laughter.
He looked from his sister to his mother, but it was
Susan he spoke to.

"You know what, Suze?"

"What?"

"You're human. For the first time in my life, you're acting human. It's great."

"Human? You want to see human?" She dipped her fingers into her water glass and splattered her brother in the face.

His eyes glowed, and he said to Rose: "This is what you get for sending your brainiac child to college for so many years."

"Hey, bro. A little birdie told me you're not doing too badly yourself."

Then Paul had interrupted the siblings, his mind evidently on matters closer to his heart. "I don't care how many people we invite, Susie, my eyes will be on you. You're beautiful even in jeans and a sweater, but can you wear one of those real wedding dresses that day? A long white one...like in the movies. It's the only wedding you and I are going to have, so you might as well knock everybody out."

Her daughter was marrying a romantic. Another Charlie. She'd loved her second dad from the start, so why not choose a guy much like him? The idea pleased Rose. It would send Charlie over the moon when she pointed it out to him.

All in all, we had a great day. Productive, too. We planned the wedding in thirty minutes. I've always been very efficient.

As if graduations and weddings weren't

enough, next Saturday night, Anita is starring in her high school's production of Bye Bye Birdie. *She's got a good little voice, with pie-in-the-sky dreams of a Broadway career. I'm keeping my mouth shut this time...except to suggest she research colleges with good theater arts programs.*

Rose yawned, folded her stationery and slipped it into the big envelope with the others. Now she could sleep.

She picked up the Dream Box and the envelope, stood and turned toward the hallway that led to the bedroom. Charlie was waiting for her.

"Reading his letters again, Rose?"

She shook her head. "Just scribbling some notes to myself, like a diary. Writing centers me. You know that, Charlie. And...and Susan had a big day." If he knew she addressed the letters to Joe, he'd think she was crazy.

She sighed. She didn't have to read Joe's letters anymore; she'd memorized them. Sadly, there weren't many—only a year's worth.

Charlie grunted, and she stroked his face. "I didn't want to disturb you, but I'm tired now, ready to sleep. Come on." She took his hand, and they walked to the bedroom.

As she lay on the bed a few minutes later, Charlie asleep beside her, she wondered for the first time if he could be jealous of a man gone for over twenty years. She discarded the thought as unworthy of Charlie.

"I'm a little nervous," said Rose as she took her seat in the high-school auditorium. Her baby had the role of Kim MacAfee, president of the Conrad Birdie Fan Club. The part was big. Demanding. Vocal and comedic.

"She'll be fine," said Charlie. "I've practiced with her. Steven's practiced with her. We've taken every part that plays against her, even sang with her. She'll break a leg."

"Ho, ho. Now you're all theater talk." She leaned over Charlie and spoke to Edith. "No matter what happens, we all applaud like crazy. Pass it down."

"Got it," said Edith. "But we're going to have a great time, Rose. Anita is Charlie's daughter. She has it all, talentwise."

The family filled up a row in the front. Gertie and Dan had driven out from the city with their three boys. Aaron, Maddy and their twin girls had come for dinner, too. The girls were just a year younger than Anita and sat on the edge of their seats looking both eager and nervous. Exactly how Rose felt.

The lights dimmed, the curtain rose and the happenings in Sweet Apple, Ohio, claimed Rose's attention. There was Anita. She played the role with everything she had to give.

Rose enjoyed the show, constantly thinking, *That's my child up there!*

It was an ensemble piece, but at the end of the evening, Rose had no doubt that Anita's performance had been the most professional—as professional as an untutored girl could give.

"Voice lessons," she murmured to Charlie. "Maybe we should give her lessons. Dancing, too. Those Broadway people can do everything."

"That's my Rosie," he said. "You say that now in the heat of the moment. Wait till tomorrow. You'll tell her to major in business so she can get a secure job in an office."

A year ago, she would have said just that, but not anymore. She glanced at Steven. He had started working with Charlie full-time and taking night classes at Queens College. He was doing well at both and was happy.

Each child was different. She'd forgotten that as they'd matured, hadn't realized that Susan's academic standards might not be right for all of them. And now, Anita had to find her own way, too. This time Rose would listen first, then offer suggestions. She was a forty-seven-year-old career woman, but not too old to learn.

To: Private Steven Shapiro, U.S. Army,
South Vietnam
June 15, 1969

Dear Steven...

Rosie's hands shook. For the past three months, she'd stumbled through the days in disbelief. *Drafted.* In the end, her worst fear had come true and her son had been drafted. He'd nodded with acceptance while she'd cried. The letter writing had begun again.

I'm glad your suspicions were right, and that you were assigned to the motor pool. I'm hoping that's a safer place to be than on roads filled with land mines.

She watched too much news on TV. Too many newsreels came out of Southeast Asia. Thickly treed jungles hid enemy troops waiting to attack. Land mines exploded seemingly at random, maiming or killing their unsuspecting victims. She wouldn't mention any of this to Steven—he knew more about it than she did. Letters from home should provide a fresh breeze, not stir up stale, hot air.

Have you been working on helicopter engines, too? I bet you'll learn to take those babies apart with no problem. You've got magic in those hands of yours, just like your dad.

Should she beg him not to smoke pot? Should

she talk about the demonstrations and draft-card burnings going on in the States? Rose rubbed her hands together and started rocking back and forth on the kitchen chair.

"No!" she finally answered herself out loud, although she was alone in the house that Saturday afternoon. "No politics."

The men in our stores ask about you all the time, and Dad and I tell them you're fine. Make sure you take care of yourself and let our answer be true. You'll be happy to know that I'm sending your drumsticks and practice pads in a separate package. I hope playing music with friends will give you a break from responsibilities. Maybe the army has a band you can join....

Hard to believe Steven was already twenty. Wasn't it only yesterday that they had celebrated his bar mitzvah? He'd still had his baby face, his smooth cheeks and high-pitched voice. She grasped her pen with both hands again.

I love you, son. You're in our thoughts and prayers every single day, every single hour. I'll write again tomorrow.
All my love, Moma

* * *

Long Island, 2007

Paul watched his mother-in-law pluck the draft notice from the Dream Box, which was now on the coffee table in the living room. Susan sat in a club chair, and Paul had planted himself behind her, his fingers playing with her hair.

"Steven spent a year in Vietnam building and taking apart all kinds of engines," Rose said from her place on the sofa. "When he first came back—" she shrugged "—he was another soldier who didn't talk much."

"He smoked a lot, though," Charlie said, walking toward Rose and sitting next to her. "I remember how the house stank with it. And he played his drums until our ears vibrated and his guitar until he got blisters."

"Finally, when he was ready, he talked," Susan said, then she immediately shook her head. "No," she amended, "he yelled. Wanted to know when I was writing a book about *his* war. I told him, I don't write about war, I write about ordinary people caught up in an extraordinary event we call war. But I couldn't do that for him because he kept everything to himself, and if he kept stonewalling me, I'd never be able to write the truth. *His* truth." She paused for a moment, then added quietly, "That's when he unloaded."

Paul, still stroking her hair, felt the shiver that ran through her from head to toe. He grasped the hand she stretched toward him. Her fingers tightened around his, and he raised them to his lips, kissing them gently.

"Unloaded. Exploded," Susan continued. "Crazy talk with no continuity. I ended up giving him a tape recorder and lots of tapes, and told him to tell me his story at his pace. Then I was able to write the articles."

"You won a prize in journalism this time," said Charlie, beaming.

"He's still as proud as a peacock," Paul whispered to Susan.

Charlie reached for a copy of the first piece in the series, "One Soldier's Story." He read Susan's words aloud: "'After serving a year in Vietnam, my little brother returned home last week. I didn't recognize him. Neither did my parents…'"

"I think you saved his sanity," Rose murmured.

"Nah. He would have been okay in time. He was just raw from the war. Actually, working with Dad was critical. So many of his buddies couldn't get jobs when they came home."

"I hired some of them," said Charlie, "but only two worked out. The others had become addicted to pot or worse. In the end, Steven found himself. He worked hard to become my partner. Then he met Pam and made us grandparents—the best reward of all."

"Absolutely," said Rose. "We are so lucky…so very, very lucky."

"My luckiest day was the day I married you,"

said Charlie. "But it wasn't until our twenty-fifth anniversary that I knew it for sure."

"That long, Dad?" teased Susan.

"I was a slow learner, Susie Q. For twenty-five years I was haunted by the notion that we'd made a mistake getting married in the first place."

Stunned, Paul could only stare at Charlie. If there was one marriage besides his own he could count on lasting, it was Rose and Charlie's.

"Wait a minute," he managed to say, picking his way through the items on the coffee table. "Here it is." He held up an invitation. "The twenty-fifth anniversary party...1971. I remember it clearly, and not only because Susie and I planned it, but because we had to keep it a secret."

Susan pointed out a framed picture of her parents on the wall. "That was taken on the night of the party. You both look great—happy—fantastic!"

"Well, sure," said Charlie. "We looked happy after Rosie and I got things settled. But just hours before, when I came home from the shops, I was anything but happy..."

Charlie felt every one of his fifty years that day. It had been a big hands-on day at CAR, Inc., because they'd been short staffed. Charlie glanced at his hands as he turned the key in the back door. Dirty nails again. Grease in his skin again. His head pounded, and the kids were throwing a party for him and Rosie that night at Edith's house. Just a small family party, they'd said, but he wasn't so sure. Paul's eyes had sparkled too much—that fine boy couldn't keep a secret. But at that moment, Charlie wished he could just lose himself in a hot bath and go to sleep.

Rose wasn't in the kitchen, and he glanced at the clock. Almost six. She was probably getting dressed for the little celebration. He hung up his jacket and walked to the back of the house.

"Rose?" he called as he entered the master bedroom.

Pen in hand, she swiveled on the desk chair, the same desk she'd brought from her parents' house in Williamsburg. The Dream Box was sitting on top of it, open, papers all around. Letters. Those damn letters.

She smiled up at him. But on this day, Charlie had had enough. "Rose," he began. "We have to talk."

It must have been his tone. Her eyes grew so big, they seemed to take up her whole face. She raced toward him. "Charlie, what's wrong? You're scaring me. Oh my God. Are you ill? Have you seen a doctor?"

"Maybe I'm ill, but a doctor can't help. Look over there," he said, pointing at the desk, "at that Dream Box you treasure. That's where Joe still lives, doesn't he? I picture him with you every time you read his letters. And each time I see you so captivated, I go away. I tell myself, respect the dead, respect her privacy, respect their love, but…"

He ran out of steam and simply shook his head. "I can't do it anymore, Rose. No more."

"But, Charlie…" she began.

He held up his hand. "Don't say anything. I'm not done." But he felt done. He wanted to sit and howl. Yet he had to finish what he'd begun here, and then…well, then they'd figure out where they stood.

He paced slowly, and Rose sat on the edge of the bed watching his every move. "When we were married, Rosie, you were honest. Joe was in your heart—your *bershert.* I knew that, but I thought, she's young, she's lovely and smart, she has to make a new life. I had enough love for both of us…at least, I thought I did.

"Somehow, though, twenty-five years have passed and here we are. Here we *still* are—you at the desk, me in the doorway. After all this time, Rosie, I have to know the truth." He took a deep breath. "Am I still second best?"

He couldn't look at her. Didn't want to see pity or sorrow. He was so tired. He dropped onto his side of the bed, leaned against the pillows and closed his eyes. Then he felt the mattress shift and knew Rose had gotten up.

Suddenly a strong breeze cooled his skin. He opened his eyes, and there was Rosie, waving sheets of paper back and forth while tears ran down her face.

"Read this, you lovable fool! I'm going to take a shower." She threw the papers at him and disappeared into the bathroom. His heart started beating again. That was Rosie. *His* Rosie. No wasted words. No wasted action.

He picked up her letter and read:

Dear Joe,

Today is my twenty-fifth wedding anniversary with Charlie, and this is my last letter to you.

In the beginning, when you went to war, we wrote to each other and prayed. Then, after I got the telegram that you died, I continued writing simply to keep myself alive, to remember why I had to go on living. In a blink, my mother and father were gone, then you, too, and I was left alone with Susan.

Then your friend came home. Thank you, Joe, for sending Charlie to me—whether you knew it or not. He changed my whole life, and I thought you should know. I wrote to you about how we were doing and how much Charlie had given to me and Susan. I also wrote to keep you alive because you fought to make our world better and never got to enjoy it. You deserved to live!

You were the first man I loved, Joe. The first man I slept with, and the father of my first child. For women, there's always a loyalty to the first love, but that doesn't mean the next love comes in second.

One morning, I woke up and knew that I loved Charlie more than I loved your memory.

Charlie's eyes refused to move farther down the page. He'd found what he'd needed to see. *She loved him.* He reread the last line and blinked away tears. He knew his wife. Her words had not been written lightly.

> *But I made a mistake. I never told Charlie how I felt. I guess I was afraid that if I told him I loved him, you would disappear from my heart altogether.*
>
> *The past twenty-five years have gone by in a day. I never thought I would love anyone else after being married to you, but how could I not fall in love with Charlie? When I die, I will spend eternity lying next to him. I hope you can understand and that we can be friends.*

Her letter ended there, which was just as well because Charlie couldn't see the words through the tears he'd finally allowed to fall. All this time she had been writing letters to Joe and not just rereading his letters? He needed to wrap his mind around that. Hell, he needed to talk to Rose.

His fatigue disappeared, and he headed toward the bathroom.

Rose stood under the hot water, reveling in its warmth; she needed it right now. Her life hung on a precipice.

The shower door opened, and there was Charlie,

naked and ready to join her. He stepped into the stall, his eyes searching her face.

"That was some letter, Rosie." His hoarse voice revealed its impact on him.

She pulled him to her. "I love you, Charlie. I've loved you for so long." She kissed him on the mouth, then kissed him again, feeling his body come alive against her.

"I knew," he murmured between touches. "I sensed it. I could tell, but I wanted to hear the words, too."

She licked his ear and whispered, "I love you, I love you, I love you..." Then she blew ever so lightly...

No more words were needed. They knew each other well. They fit each other well, this time against a wet wall under running water. A renewed passion surfaced as she looked at her husband, her lover, this good man who'd showered her with love from the beginning.

She stood on her toes, her hands on his shoulders as she faced him, wriggling until she caught him, tightening her legs and holding him at just the right spot. Little by little, she pulsed back and forth until he filled her.

Holding each other, they found their rhythm. A new, wild rhythm. She danced to a syncopated drumbeat. Free! Free to be herself.

She tingled everywhere his hand touched, but it was Charlie who gasped, "Rosie! I can't hold out, I can't..."

"Yes!"

And they were one.

Together they collapsed to the floor on rubbery legs, limbs entangled, trying to breathe, trying to come back to life.

Charlie stroked her cheek. "This part of our lives always kept me hoping for the rest."

She kissed him. "Of course I love you."

"Of course?" he teased. "There's no of course about it. What you usually say, Rosie, is, 'Charlie, you're such a good man.' Or 'Sleep tight, dear.' That's not the same thing at all."

He reached up and turned off the spigots.

"But haven't we built a wonderful life together, Charlie?"

"The best." He hoisted himself up and reached for her hand. "Come on. We're going to celebrate tonight…hmm…let's say, *add* to the celebration." He grinned at her, and she thought he looked like he did twenty-five years ago. Only better.

"Charlie," she said, standing and stroking his cheek. "Maybe it was us. Maybe we're the ones…?"

His eyes widened. "The ones…who were meant to be?"

"*Bershert,*" she whispered.

"I'm not going to argue." He toweled her off instead and laughed. "Rosie, you're my practical woman with a most romantic streak."

Chapter 14

Thirty-five years later, Rose still wasn't sure she had a romantic streak. On the other hand, she had planned a surprise for Charlie for their sixtieth anniversary the next night that would knock him out. Her excitement grew each time she thought about the celebration, and she turned to hide her smile because he still sat next to her on the couch. Maybe she did harbor a romantic soul after all.

But she hadn't changed her mind about the kids. Lizzy and Matthew didn't have to know the details of their grandparents' first twenty-five years, not when that darling boy was on the verge of going to war and leaving his pregnant wife alone.

Charlie looked at Susan and said, "That letter was the last letter your mother wrote to Joe."

"I understand," said Susan. "You had to live your real lives fully and openly, and go forward."

"By then the pieces finally fit together," added Rose. "Do you remember the next year when we all went to Europe? To the American cemetery in Belgium where Joe rests?"

"Of course, I remember," Susan said. "Near Liège. It was the most important trip I've ever taken." She looked at her mother. "Visiting Daddy Joe provided closure for me. I can't thank you enough for taking us." She left her chair and gave Rose, then Charlie, a hug. "You guys have been the best parents anyone could have. I wish…I wish I were as good. I've screwed up with Lizzy and Matt, and now I have to fix it."

"You will," said Rose. "It's amazing how powerful an 'I love you' can be. Or an 'I'm sorry.'"

"I'll help you," said Paul.

But Susan shook her head. "You didn't mess up. I did."

"We're in this life together," he replied. "Just like your folks." Paul extended his hand to Susan. "Come on, Suze. It's time to go home." She clasped it and rose from her chair.

Paul kissed Rose, clapped Charlie on the shoulder. "Everyone loves you guys. You'll see proof of that tomorrow night at the temple."

"The temple? But the party's at your house, Paul," Rose protested, staring at her daughter.

"A little change in venue," Susan replied quickly. "I didn't think you'd mind. It was, hmm… easier for me."

"Oh. Of course," Rose said slowly. "It's just that I thought I was in charge."

"Oh, you are, Mom. Definitely. With a few little additions and changes." Susan winked and disappeared, Paul right behind her.

"What did they mean?" asked Rose.

Charlie shrugged.

"Darn it!" she said. "I still don't like surprises."

Charlie laughed, shook his head, looked at Rose and laughed some more.

But he found nothing funny the next evening when he spotted his tuxedo hanging on the door.

"I'm not wearing the monkey suit!" he said, walking into the bedroom closet. "There's nothing wrong with my good blue one."

Rose groaned. "You're not going to the bank, Charlie. Besides, you'll look so handsome in those elegant clothes. You can still do yourself proud—and me, too."

When she squeezed his shoulder, he reached for the tux. Still vain enough to want to look good. Still in love enough to want to please her.

Ten minutes later, he was dressed and ready when the doorbell rang, the sound quickly followed by the rise and fall of excited young voices. "Lizzy and Matt are here. Our chauffeurs are early," he said, poking his head into the bedroom.

"Good. You talk to them. I need another minute."

"No you don't. You're perfect."

"I love you, Charlie."

"Yeah...I know." He kissed her and went to greet the children.

Rose stood in front of her full-length mirror. The ivory suit with its long skirt was reminiscent of a wedding and fit beautifully. Pearl-and-diamond drop earrings framed her face; a rope of pearls with a diamond clasp hung from her neck. On her left hand, she wore her everyday plain gold wedding band, the one piece of jewelry that really counted. She stroked it gently.

As she stared, a satisfied smile peeked back at her. Charlie would be so pleased later when he realized what she had arranged. She grabbed her purse, checked the contents and left the solitude of the bedroom, ready to take on the world. Her world.

She didn't expect the sound of hushed voices in the living room. Three focused people, with serious expressions, turned toward her in unison when she entered the room. "What's going on?"

"Gram, you look gorgeous!"

But it was Liz who looked beautiful in a royal-blue crepe dress that hid her rounded stomach, and Matthew who was as handsome as a young wife could wish. The kids were dressed for a party, but certainly didn't seem to be in a party mood.

Charlie answered her question. "How'd you like to have a full guest room for the next year?"

It didn't take a genius to figure out what was transpiring. "Lizzy? You want to stay with us while Matt's away?"

Liz shook her head. "I'm perfectly capable of taking care of myself."

"I'd feel better if she were staying with family, mainly because of the baby, while I'm gone," Matt admitted. "And this house always feels like home."

The young man looked so eager, so hopeful that Rose couldn't breathe for a moment. "Lizzy is welcome here anytime, for as long as she wants. You are, too, Matthew."

Rose cleared her throat. "Have you mentioned this idea to your mother, Liz?"

Storm clouds gathered. "She'll find out soon enough."

It will break her heart, but Rose said nothing more. This was between Susan and Liz, and Susan would have to handle it.

Rose turned to Charlie. "Are you ready to celebrate?"

"Always." He took her hand and they followed their grandchildren to the car.

They entered the parking lot of Temple Sinai fifteen minutes later. Rose and Charlie had been part of the congregation since their move to Long Island more than forty years earlier. The parking lot was almost full, and Rose turned to Charlie.

"Charlie, what have you done? I didn't include this many people on the guest list."

"Me? I haven't done anything. This was your idea."

"No wonder Susan said it would be easier. Lizzy! What's going on?"

Her granddaughter turned around in the front seat and grinned. "I see no evil. Hear no evil. Speak no evil," she said. "I'm sworn to secrecy."

"I don't like surprises," Rose mumbled, "unless I'm springing them."

Charlie held her arm as they walked to the front door of the brick building, Liz and Matt behind them. Matt was on his cell phone. Rose glanced at her husband, illuminated by the streetlamps. His eyes were sparkling, his expression eager. She'd seen that look so many times in the past. The man was ready for a good time.

Well, darn it. So was she!

When they walked through the door, she heard "The Yellow Rose of Texas" while the photographer snapped their pictures. Susan stood beyond the man's shoulder, a wide smile lighting her face. "Professional is better," she said.

"Wow!" said Charlie. "Oh, my. Look, Rosie! There's Hank Johnson all the way from Iowa. He's using a cane, but he got here. Did you invite him? We should have picked him up at the airport."

"No," she whispered. "I never thought...I planned smaller..."

An hour later, Rose understood that Susan's invitation list went far beyond Gertie's and Aaron's families and all the offspring and spouses. It went beyond the close friends in the neighborhood and CAR employees. And her daughter had never said a word.

But now it was time to spring her surprise. Rose

scanned the social hall for Rabbi Bernstein and nodded at him.

The rabbi took the microphone. "Ladies and gentlemen," he began, "sixty years ago, Rose and Charlie Shapiro got married in a very simple ceremony witnessed by only a few people. Times were hard after the war, and their particular circumstances were difficult. Therefore, at Rose's request, today we have gathered not only to celebrate Rose and Charlie's sixtieth wedding anniversary, but to witness them renewing their vows of marriage under the chuppah in the sanctuary. Please make your way there now."

An excited hum passed through the room, and their guests immediately followed the rabbi's directions.

Charlie's legs were planted on the floor. "Renew our vows, Rosie? Does that mean another sixty years together?"

"And what's wrong with that, old man?" snapped Rose, her expression warm.

"Not a single thing. Come on, let's give folks something to think about."

"I already wrote down what I want to say." She reached into her evening bag for the sheet of paper. "I'm pretty sure you'll like it, and then you can say it back to me."

"I'd be delighted."

"Charles Shapiro," she read, "it was sixty years ago that I pledged my love and commitment to you, but it seems like only yesterday. Under the chuppah,

I promised to love, honor and cherish you, to be by your side in sickness and health, for better or worse for the rest of our lives. We have had all those things, and you have been by my side as we raised our three children and created a life together.

"Today, as we begin our sixty-first year as husband and wife, in the presence of God, and our family and friends, I renew my vows to you, pledging my eternal love and eagerly awaiting what life may yet bring us."

What life may yet bring us...

The words repeated themselves in Susan's mind, her attention split between the festivities and her children. Life was bringing Lizzy and Matt both joy and heartache. She'd experienced the gamut herself, real life-and-death heartache, but she would rather face it herself again than watch her children go through it. That wasn't realistic, however. Each person traveled his or her own journey.

She poured a glass of wine, and with a determined tread, walked to the bandstand as the group finished a session. She took the microphone with her free hand and waited until people had returned to their tables, making sure Liz and Matt were seated at theirs.

"It seems that my family is full of announcements and celebrations these days," she began, pausing until she had everyone's attention. "So, at this time, I invite you all to join me in a salute to my son-in-law, Matthew Solomon, who will soon be serving our country in the Middle East, bringing his healing skills to those who will most need them." She raised her glass and caught Matt's eye. "To Matthew, a man of highest honor." Then she mouthed, *Please forgive me.*

A wide grin crossed Matt's face. He not only stood, but immediately approached and led her back to Lizzy.

"I was going to stay with Grandma and Papa while Matt was away, but if it's okay, I'd like to live with you and Dad instead," said Liz.

"You're making your mother cry," said Paul softly. "But it's a good cry."

When the band returned, Liz and Matt stepped onto the dance floor. They were not alone.

"Just look at my grandparents," said Liz, glancing at Rose and Charlie. "They're so perfect together. In every way. I can't imagine her with anyone else, not even with my natural grandfather, Grandpa Joe."

"That was way before your time," said Matt.

"I know. And he was such a short part of her life…married only about six months before he shipped out. Gram probably doesn't even think about him after all these years."

Suddenly her husband's mouth was on hers, his kiss hard and provocative, his arms embracing her tightly. "God, I hope you're wrong," he said.

"Because I'll love you forever, Liz. Throughout eternity. No matter what happens."

In that moment, everything changed for Liz. "Oh, Matt. Of course, of course. I'll love you, too, no matter what." She snuggled against him, then peered at Rose once more. What stories she could tell. But her grandmother simply waved at her and smiled.

Charlie watched them all. Whether on the dance floor or at the tables, he watched the big dramas. The small dramas. Susan. Steven. Anita. Friends. Family. His family, without whom life would mean nothing.

He walked toward an open door. He'd danced all evening, and fresh air beckoned. Standing on the threshold, he took a deep breath and tilted his head back. Stars twinkled in an unclouded sky.

You're going to be a great-grandpa, Joe, and everything will be okay. "For as many years as remain to me," he murmured. Satisfied, he glanced into the building and saw Matt in conversation with Paul. *The home front is in good hands.*

Charlie inhaled deeply, then listened hard. The music had started up again. Time to find Rosie.

When he returned to the dance floor, the band began playing his and Rosie's song. Taking her into his arms, she felt as lithe as ever, and if their step was a little slower, it didn't matter. As long as he danced with his Rosie.

Automatically he began to sing, "'Hold me close

and hold me fast…'" The music softened until it was mere background noise. He still carried a tune, not as strong as once upon a time, but not too bad either….

He sang the song through, and when he finished, the sound of applause broke his reverie. He and Rose stood in the center of a circle, a circle of family and friends that had begun so long ago and had grown until this very day. There was only one thing for him to do now.

Charlie Shapiro leaned down and kissed his bride.

* * * * *

SPECIAL EDITION®

LIFE, LOVE AND FAMILY

*These contemporary romances will strike
a chord with you as heroines juggle life and
relationships on their way to true love.*

New York Times *bestselling author*
Linda Lael Miller brings you a
BRAND-NEW contemporary story featuring
her fan-favorite McKettrick family.

Meg McKettrick is surprised to be reunited
with her high-school flame, Brad O'Ballivan.
After enjoying a career as a country-and-western
singer, Brad aches for a home and family…
and seeing Meg again makes him realize he
still loves her. But their pride manages to interfere with love…until an unexpected match-
maker gets involved.

Turn the page for a sneak preview of
THE McKETTRICK WAY
by Linda Lael Miller.
On sale November 20,
wherever books are sold.

Brad shoved the truck into gear and drove to the bottom of the hill, where the road forked. Turn left, and he'd be home in five minutes. Turn right, and he was headed for Indian Rock.

He had no damn business going to Indian Rock.

He had nothing to say to Meg McKettrick, and if he never set eyes on the woman again, it would be two weeks too soon.

He turned right.

He couldn't have said why.

He just drove straight to the Dixie Dog Drive-In.

Back in the day, he and Meg used to meet at the Dixie Dog, by tacit agreement, when either of them had been away. It had been some kind of universe thing, purely intuitive.

Passing familiar landmarks, Brad told himself he ought to turn around. The old days were gone. Things had ended badly between him and Meg anyhow, and she wasn't going to be at the Dixie Dog.

He kept driving.

He rounded a bend, and there was the Dixie Dog. Its big neon sign, a giant hot dog, was all lit up and going through its corny sequence—first it was covered in red squiggles of light, meant to suggest ketchup, and then yellow, for mustard.

Brad pulled into one of the slots next to a speaker, rolled down the truck window and ordered.

A girl roller-skated out with the order about five minutes later.

When she wheeled up to the driver's window, smiling, her eyes went wide with recognition, and she dropped the tray with a clatter.

Silently Brad swore. Damn if he hadn't forgotten he was a famous country singer.

The girl, a skinny thing wearing too much eye makeup, immediately started to cry. "I'm sorry!" she sobbed, squatting to gather up the mess.

"It's okay," Brad answered quietly, leaning to look down at her, catching a glimpse of her plastic name tag. "It's okay, Mandy. No harm done."

"I'll get you another dog and a shake right away, Mr. O'Ballivan!"

"Mandy?"

She stared up at him pitifully, sniffling. Thanks to the copious tears, most of the goop on her eyes had slid south. "Yes?"

"When you go back inside, could you not mention seeing me?"

"But you're Brad O'Ballivan!"

"Yeah," he answered, suppressing a sigh. "I know."

She rolled a little closer. "You wouldn't happen to have a picture you could autograph for me, would you?"

"Not with me," Brad answered.

"You could sign this napkin, though," Mandy said. "It's only got a little chocolate on the corner."

Brad took the paper napkin and her order pen, and scrawled his name. Handed both items back through the window.

She turned and whizzed back toward the side entrance to the Dixie Dog.

Brad waited, marveling that he hadn't considered incidents like this one before he'd decided to come back home. In retrospect, it seemed shortsighted, to say the least, but the truth was, he'd expected to be—Brad O'Ballivan.

Presently Mandy skated back out again, and this time she managed to hold on to the tray.

"I didn't tell a soul!" she whispered. "But Heather and Darlene *both* asked me why my mascara was all smeared." Efficiently she hooked the tray onto the bottom edge of the window.

Brad extended payment, but Mandy shook her head.

"The boss said it's on the house, since I dumped your first order on the ground."

He smiled. "Okay, then. Thanks."

Mandy retreated, and Brad was just reaching for the food when a bright red Blazer whipped into the space beside his. The driver's door sprang open, crashing into the metal speaker, and somebody got out in a hurry.

Something quickened inside Brad.

And in the next moment Meg McKettrick was standing practically on his running board, her blue eyes blazing.

Brad grinned. "I guess you're not over me after all," he said.

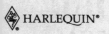

REQUEST YOUR FREE BOOKS!

2 FREE NOVELS PLUS 2 FREE GIFTS!

 HARLEQUIN®

E V E R L A S T I N G   L O V E ™

Every great love has a story to tell™

YES! Please send me 2 FREE Harlequin® Everlasting Love™ novels and my 2 FREE gifts. After receiving them, if I don't wish to receive any more books, I can return the shipping statement marked "cancel." If I don't cancel, I will receive 4 brand-new novels every other month and be billed just $4.47 per book in the U.S. or $4.99 per book in Canada, plus 25¢ shipping and handling per book and applicable taxes, if any*. That's a savings of about 15% off the cover price! I understand that accepting the 2 free books and gifts places me under no obligation to buy anything. I can always return a shipment and cancel at any time. Even if I never buy another book from Harlequin, the two free books and gifts are mine to keep forever.

153 HDN ELX4 353 HDN ELYG

Name	(PLEASE PRINT)	
Address		Apt.
City	State/Prov.	Zip/Postal Code

Signature (if under 18, a parent or guardian must sign)

Mail to the **Harlequin Reader Service®:**
IN U.S.A.: P.O. Box 1867, Buffalo, NY 14240-1867
IN CANADA: P.O. Box 609, Fort Erie, Ontario L2A 5X3

Not valid to current Harlequin Everlasting Love subscribers.

Want to try two free books from another line?
Call 1-800-873-8635 or visit www.morefreebooks.com.

* Terms and prices subject to change without notice. NY residents add applicable sales tax. Canadian residents will be charged applicable provincial taxes and GST. This offer is limited to one order per household. All orders subject to approval. Credit or debit balances in a customer's account(s) may be offset by any other outstanding balance owed by or to the customer. Please allow 4 to 6 weeks for delivery.

Your Privacy: Harlequin is committed to protecting your privacy. Our Privacy Policy is available online at www.eHarlequin.com or upon request from the Reader Service. From time to time we make our lists of customers available to reputable firms who may have a product or service of interest to you. If you would prefer we not share your name and address, please check here. ☐

HEL07

Inside ROMANCE

Stay up-to-date on all your
romance reading news!

Inside Romance is a FREE quarterly newsletter
highlighting our upcoming series releases
and promotions.

Visit

www.eHarlequin.com/InsideRomance

to sign up to receive our complimentary newsletter today!

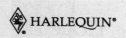

HARLEQUIN®

American ★ Romance®

Kate Merrill had grown up convinced
that the most attractive men were incapable
of ever settling down. Yet the harder she
resisted the superstar photographer
Tyler Nichols, the more persistent the
handsome world traveler became.
So by the time Christmas arrived, there
was only one wish on her holiday list—
that she was wrong!

LOOK FOR

THE CHRISTMAS DATE

BY

Michele Dunaway

Available December
wherever you buy books

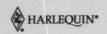

COMING NEXT MONTH

#21 CHRISTMAS PRESENTS AND PAST
by Janice Kay Johnson

My true love gave to me... Every Christmas gift Will and Dinah exchange is a symbol of their love. The tradition begins on their very first date, when Will arrives with an exquisitely wrapped present, and it continues every holiday season thereafter—whether they're together or apart—until something in their lives goes very wrong. And then only an unexpected gift can make things right.

#22 A SPIRIT OF CHRISTMAS by Margot Early

A modern retelling of Dickens's *A Christmas Carol*. It is said that Keti and Martin Collins keep Christmas very well. But it wasn't always this way.... Despite—or perhaps because of—Martin Collins, the man she's always loved but couldn't marry, Keti Whitechapel had a "Bah, humbug" attitude toward life. But one Christmas Eve, Keti finds a dog she names Marley. That night she has a dream about Christmas past. And Christmas present—and future. A future that could include the man she's loved all these years...

www.eHarlequin.com

HECNM1107